**"Let me help," Laredo said, already out of his truck.**

He took her two bags, leaving Mary free to return for Lark. "Hope you don't mind," he said, "but I grabbed the base from your baby's carrier out of your car. I know we're only going a short way but figured it's always best to err on the side of caution."

"True. Thanks."

He opened the passenger-side door. "Let me help. It's a high reach." Taking the baby's carrier from her, he soon had it snapped into the base. "All set."

"How do you know so much about baby equipment? It took me a few weeks to perfect that move."

"Long story with no good answer."

Okay, could he be more cryptic? Didn't matter, since after about ten minutes, they'd never see each other again.

Besides, she had her own secrets.

He was entitled to his.

Dear Reader,

When I was a teen, every Thursday night my grandfather set up a card table in the kitchen next to the house's only phone, which was a wall-mounted landline. For you youngins, that's how we lived in the olden days! LOL! Grandma carefully set out pens and paper and a list of scripts she was to use for various heartbreaking situations.

You see, once a week she volunteered to take calls from the battered-women shelter in Fayetteville, Arkansas. I'm sure it now has a fancier name, but tragically, the issues are still the same. According to the National Coalition Against Domestic Violence, NCADV.org, the following grim statistics show that women—and men—are still being abused in their own homes.

On average, nearly twenty people per minute are abused by an intimate partner in the United States.

On a typical day, there are more than twenty thousand phone calls placed to domestic violence hotlines nationwide.

**If you are in immediate danger, call 9-1-1.**
**For anonymous, confidential help, 24/7,**
**please call the National Domestic Violence Hotline at 1-800-799-7233 (SAFE) or 1-800-787-3224 (TTY).**
**Most important, know that abuse is not your fault!**

Though Robin and Laredo struggle for their second chance at love, my wish for all of my awesome readers is that love finds you as easily as a warm summer breeze.

Warmest regards,

*Laura Marie* xoxo

HOME *on the* RANCH

# COLORADO COWBOY SEAL

LAURA MARIE ALTOM

HARLEQUIN® HOME ON THE RANCH

Recycling programs
for this product may
not exist in your area.

ISBN-13: 978-1-335-00558-8
ISBN-13: 978-1-335-63393-4 (Direct to Consumer edition)

Home on the Ranch: Colorado Cowboy SEAL



This edition published by arrangement with Harlequin Books S.A.

For questions and comments about the quality of this book, please contact us at CustomerService@Harlequin.com.

**Printed in U.S.A.**

**Laura Marie Altom** is a bestselling and award-winning author who has penned nearly fifty books. After college—go, Hogs!—Laura Marie did a brief stint as an interior designer before becoming a stay-at-home mom to boy-girl twins and a bonus son. Always an avid romance reader, she knew it was time to try her hand at writing when she found herself replotting the afternoon soaps.

When not immersed in her next story, Laura plays video games, tackles Mount Laundry and, of course, reads romance!

Laura loves hearing from readers either at PO Box 2074, Tulsa, OK 74101, or by email, balipalm@aol.com.

Love winning fun stuff? Check out lauramariealtom.com.

**Books by Laura Marie Altom**

**Harlequin Western Romance**

***Cowboy SEALs***

*The SEAL's Miracle Baby*
*The Baby and the Cowboy SEAL*
*The SEAL's Second Chance Baby*
*The Cowboy SEAL's Jingle Bell Baby*
*The Cowboy SEAL's Christmas Baby*
*Cowboy SEAL Daddy*

Visit the Author Profile page
at Harlequin.com for more titles.

For all domestic violence survivors. You deserve the happiest of new beginnings... xoxo

# Chapter 1

"Help! *Please!* He's got my baby!"

Newly retired Navy SEAL, Laredo "Lion" Tucker, squinted against the setting August sun's glare, removing the gas nozzle from his more-rust-than-red Ford truck. What the hell?

Hand to his forehead, shading his eyes, it took two seconds to realize the woman at the next pump was being carjacked. An infant seat was visible through the white Focus's rear window.

California plates.

The guy doing the jacking had hold of the hysterical woman, wrestling her from the running vehicle before shoving her to the truck stop's concrete lot.

Not thinking, just doing, pulse pounding with adrenaline he hadn't felt since combat, Laredo reached through his truck's open window for his crossbow. Before the jacker drove more than twenty yards toward the desolate, two-lane state highway, Laredo shot the car's left rear tire, then the right. Though the guy had gunned the engine, the four-cylinder couldn't have been going much over thirty miles per hour when the tires blew.

The vehicle fishtailed onto the dusty adjoining lot. The force killed the motor.

Time stood still.

Above the omnipresent wind's lonely wail rose the baby's cries.

Crossbow at his side, Laredo charged across the lot.

By the time the thug jumped from the driver's-side door, Laredo flung his bow to the weeds, then pummeled the guy with a hard left to his jaw. The jacker held a gun but tumbled backward.

The cheap 9 mm fell harmlessly to the ground.

Wrenching the guy's arms behind him, Laredo flipped him onto his belly, pinning him to the ground with a knee to the center of his lower back. Laredo slid off his leather belt, wrapping it around the man's wrists.

During the chase and ensuing capture, Laredo had been so hyperfocused on saving the screaming woman's baby, he hadn't noticed the citizen army gathering behind him.

An approaching siren's wail cut the animated crowd's chatter. Red-and-blue lights stole twilight's usual peace. For the plains of Dandelion Gulch, Colorado, this was some crazy excitement of the sort Laredo was damned glad they didn't see every day.

Lulu—the truck stop's owner—had been kind enough to wrap a blanket around the infant's sobbing mother's shoulders while leading her across the lot toward her baby. Though the air was warm, she shivered. Shock?

Laredo hefted the carjacking bastard onto his feet,

shoving him toward a half-dozen angry locals. "Would y'all mind looking after this piece of shit till the sheriff can deal with him."

They were all too happy to oblige.

"Oh—and once he's cuffed, kindly get my belt." Laredo opened the rear door to rescue the bawling infant.

*"Waaaahuh! Waaaaahuh!"*

"Shh…" As gingerly as possible with his meaty hands, Laredo lifted the tiny pink bundle from her safety seat, then cradled her to his chest. "It's okay, little lady. Your mama's on her way."

"H-how can I ever thank you?" The petite brunette with big brown eyes didn't try hiding free-flowing tears.

"No thanks necessary, ma'am." Over a foot taller than her, he had to duck to pass the baby into her waiting arms. The sight of the reunited mother and child should have been enchanting. Instead, it felt like a fist to his gut.

A reminder of what might've been.

"You dropped this." Lulu handed him his brown leather cowboy hat. "It fell off while you were running."

"I didn't notice." Laredo wiped the forearm of his long-sleeve denim shirt across his brow, then slapped the hat back on his head. "Thanks."

"My pleasure, cowboy." It was no secret the bottle-blond owner had a thing for him, but he wasn't in the market for anything she—or any woman—had to offer.

The crowd followed the action, meaning everyone save for Lulu left as soon as the citizen militia took the car-jacker to where the sheriff had parked near the pumps.

"Where were you headed?" he asked the woman with the baby.

"South."

"Hmm." He might be a retired Navy SEAL, but that

didn't mean there wasn't enough of the highly trained soldier left in him to suspect there was a whole lot more the woman wasn't saying. "I guess before we get you back on your way, even if I put on your spare, you'll need another new tire and spare. There's a repair shop down the road. I'll—"

"How much will that cost?" Her gaze welled with fresh tears.

"Tell you what, since I was the one who wrecked them, I suppose it should be me buying the new ones."

"I couldn't accept that large of a gift."

"It wouldn't be a gift, but me making good. In the meantime, let's get you a place to stay. There's a motel not too far from the repair shop. I'll get you a room."

"Thanks, but I'll stay with my car."

"With all due respect, I'm pretty sure Jimmy's—the repair shop—is closed till morning. That's why I suggested the room. If cost is an issue, I'll cover that, too." Before joining the Navy, he'd known tough times. A quick appraisal showed the woman dressed well enough. Black leather boots into which she'd tucked the hems of hip-hugging designer jeans. Her pale V-necked sweater lent the impression of expensive softness. A wild tumble of thick dark hair framed her pretty face. No makeup, but even her smooth complexion read the kind of money it took for fancy department store lotions.

On the other hand, her car didn't.

And maybe he was overanalyzing when the good Lord had merely blessed her with unblemished skin. Maybe Laredo had spent too much time focused on terrorists and not enough on the kinds of things that gave a man the deep-down satisfaction he'd never found.

In another place and time, he might have seen himself holding the woman's petite frame, skimming his fingers over her hair while whispering words of comfort.

Now, all he was capable of feeling was numb.

"I've got an idea," Lulu said, having watched the exchange with one perfectly arched eyebrow raised. "Ma'am, I'm sure Kyle—our sheriff—will want to question you. How about you relax in our best corner booth till Laredo finds out about the tire. Maybe Jimmy will still be at his shop and do a rush job for you."

"Yes," the stranger said with a halting nod. "That sounds good. But no need to bother the sheriff since he already has the bad guy. Thanks—to both of you."

"No problem, sugar." The woman put her arm around the mother and her child, turning her toward the truck stop's entrance. "Laredo, hon, how about you grab her purse and any baby gear from her car?"

"I'll get all of that." The woman lurched free from Lulu to angle back toward her crippled ride.

She marched toward her car with what Laredo could only describe as a sort of desperation not to have him touch her belongings.

On instinct, he backed away, holding out his hands palms up to prove he was no threat.

Keeping one eye on him, she fished in the back seat for a diaper bag. Rounding the car, she took her purse and a small duffel bag from the passenger side before slamming the door. Including the baby, she held more than a good pack mule.

"I'm Laredo," he said to put her at ease, or if not that, to at least be neighborly. "Let me lighten your load." He took the diaper bag and duffel. "Navy friends call me Lion. Both names suck, but my mother was homesick for Texas back when she delivered me on Guam. Dad was stationed there. My SEAL brothers gave me the other one during hell week and it stuck."

"You never mentioned that to me," Lulu said.

Funny, Laredo had forgotten the truck stop's owner and waitress was still there. He was transfixed by the sight of this doe-eyed stranger and her baby. He typically didn't say a whole lot, but the timid beauty had him babbling like a brook.

"I'm Lulu." The truck stop's owner held out her hand to the woman. "Seeing how we're all getting to know each other, what's your name?"

The stranger seemed caught off guard by the question. But then she half smiled. "I'm Mary Smith."

Right. And he was next in line for the presidency.

"Well, Mary." Lulu wrapped her arm around the woman's shoulders. "I'm awfully sorry to be meeting under these circumstances, but around here, we take care of our own. Let's get you and your baby settled with coffee and a nice piece of Cook's famous chocolate pie, then you can fill in the sheriff on exactly what happened."

Mary shook her head, but then nodded.

Watching the women leave, Laredo slowly exhaled.

The fairer sex made him feel about as lost as last year's Easter eggs. It had been about Easter of last year when his life had gone to hell in a basket.

As soon as Laredo ensured Lulu and Mary were safely inside, he set their gear alongside the booth, then hopped in his truck for the short ride into town.

The sun had almost tucked itself in, casting an orange, red and yellow net over the barren land Laredo called home. When he'd bought his ranch here, it had been a dream come true. A way to calm the demons a decade of war and the wrong gal had left in his heart.

With wide-open skies and tall grasses that on a cloudless day resembled a vast inland sea, Laredo was here to heal.

His encounter with Mary may be counterproductive to that goal, but it wasn't like he'd had a choice. The woman had needed him, and though he may have traded his SEAL Trident for a tractor, that didn't mean he wouldn't always be first to lend a hand when needed.

Jimmy Schmidt's repair shop was just past the feed store.

Sadly, as Laredo had suspected, the place was shut down for the night. Jimmy's fiancée was planning the Halloween wedding of the decade and she kept her man on a tight leash. No doubt he was home tying candy corn bags or helping with the seating plan. She said his handwriting wasn't good enough to help with invitations.

Since replacement tires were no longer on the agenda, Laredo figured he'd best rent Mary a room at the town's only motel—The Lonely Cactus Motor Court. The task took all of five minutes. Once he'd pocketed the old-fashioned key that dangled by a plastic cowboy boot, he reluctantly climbed back behind his truck's wheel to break the bad news to Mary and hand over the key to her home for the night.

Ten minutes later, the sky had grown a little too dark for his liking. It would be a long ride home.

Laredo entered the truck stop's diner to find it still hopping. Business hadn't been this good since the last blizzard when Lulu's was the only place in town with a satellite signal strong enough to catch the Super Bowl.

George Strait crooned on the jukebox and on the big-screen TV the Cubs beat the Cardinals.

Laredo scanned the rowdy crowd to find Mary and her baby holding court in the big corner booth. Knowing he was on a deadline to get home, the last thing he wanted was to enter the fray, but he did need to give Mary her room key.

He would have expected a woman in her situation to be relieved. Maybe talkative from the adrenaline rush and resulting relief of a potentially catastrophic situation taking a good turn. Instead, she sat with her head bowed, clutching her baby.

Maybe she was still in shock?

"There he is!" Sheriff Kyle Marsh waved him over. Kyle had been a Marine, so the two of them had long since bonded over military service and venison jerky recipes. Kyle stood, meeting Laredo midway to the booth to shake his hand. "Our hero! What the hell? You're making me look bad in front of my constituents."

"All twenty of them?" Laredo and Kyle shared a laugh.

"Always bustin' my balls. Slide in here and have a piece of pie on me. You've earned it."

"Stop." After easing into the booth seat, Laredo clasped his hands on the table. "I did what anyone else would have. It wasn't a big deal."

"Turns out it was." Lulu put her left hand atop his right.

He tried casually extricating his digits, but the woman had an iron grip. He didn't want to make a scene but it looked like he and the buxom truck stop owner needed to have a serious talk.

He glanced across the table to find Mary eyeing him and Lulu. He didn't want Mary getting the wrong impression about the two of them being an item. On the flip side, he wasn't sure why it mattered. But it did. Which was even more unsettling than Lulu's proprietary hold.

"Kyle, do you want to share the big news, or shall I?"

"Go for it," Kyle said.

"Well…" Lulu paused for dramatic effect. "Turns out Mary's carjacker was a felon. His name is John Paul Matthews and he's wanted for a whole slew of convenience store robberies down in Louisiana. How he found his way up here, I'll never know, but thank goodness we have our very own big, strong Navy SEAL to help out when the sheriff isn't around."

"I'm retired," Laredo said.

"Once a SEAL, always a SEAL." Kyle tipped his beer to him. "Face it, you're a hero. My deputy took Mr. Matthews to a nice, comfy cell, so now all we need to worry about is getting Miss Smith's car back on the road."

"Working on it." Laredo fished the motel room key from his jeans pocket, then slid it across the brown laminate table past coffee cups and saucers filled with piecrust crumbs. "No tires tonight, Mary, but I got you a room. I'll run you over as soon as you're ready."

She frowned. "We already talked about this."

"Look…" He leaned in. "Your car is currently in a field. You've been through a traumatic event and you and your baby need a safe, quiet place to grab some shut-eye. I already paid for the room. You're not in any way beholden to me. But I do feel bad about your tires."

"You saved my baby's life. You've done enough."

"Honey," Lulu said, "take the room."

Mary nodded. "Thanks."

"Come on." Laredo rose from the booth. "I'll give you a ride."

"That's okay," Lulu said. "I'll be happy to drive her. I haven't visited with Sarah in ages." Sarah Ziegler had taken over the motel when her parents retired to Arizona. Luckily, she hadn't been on duty when Laredo booked the room.

Dandelion Gulch was a hotbed of single women on the prowl for potential husbands.

"Sounds good. I'll hit up Jimmy first thing in the morning about the tires." Laredo limited trips to town in hopes of staying off the groom candidate roster. It sucked that he'd have to make a return trip tomorrow, but he'd deal. His more pressing issue was getting safely home tonight. "Mary? You okay with this plan?"

"Yes. Thank you. You're very kind."

Laredo winced.

Actually, he was a selfish bastard for resenting the time this stranger had already unwittingly taken from his day. And tomorrow. His whole point for leaving the Navy and moving to this lonely corner of the world was to escape. Hide. But none of that was feasible when he was surrounded by flirting women and now a random violent crime.

"See y'all in the morning." With a backward wave, he retreated from the diner.

Unfortunately, the sound of clicking heels followed.

"Not so fast, cowboy." Lulu passed, cutting him off before he reached the door. "I wanted to thank you for helping with this fiasco. It's not every day a man literally tackles a criminal while helping a lady in distress."

"No problem."

"Yes, but—"

"I don't mean to be rude," he said, "but I've got even more ladies in distress back home. If I don't feed my hens, they'll bust into the house and peck me to death in my sleep."

Lulu laughed. "You're so funny." Hand on his forearm, she added, "Just know that if you ever find yourself needing a favor from me—*anything at all*—I'm here for you. It must get lonely out there on your ranch, and a man has needs that—"

"Whoa." He lowered his voice, ensuring no one else could hear. "Hon, you are a smart, savvy businesswoman and just about the hottest firecracker any man could hold, but I'm not in the market, okay?"

"I'm confused. Do you bat for the other team? If so, I could hook you up with—"

He sighed. "Nothing personal, but I really just want to be left alone."

Making the already awkward moment all the more difficult was Mary. Laredo glanced up, accidentally catching her gaze. In the moment, she looked as hollow as he felt.

What was her story?

Why did he care?

"I know you don't mean any of that," Lulu said. "I understand that as a proud man who's served our country, you've seen things I can't even imagine. But that doesn't mean—"

"I'll see you the next time I get a hankering for meat loaf." In case of crocodile tears, Laredo took off, punching open the door with its chirpy bell, then making a beeline for his truck.

Thankfully, Lulu and her heels didn't follow.

What did?

Mary Smith's haunted expression.

# Chapter 2

Robin woke unsure where she was.

*Who she was.*

Heart pounding, it took her minute to realize she was safe. No one here knew her real name, and as long as she remained Mary Smith to them, all would be well. She was safe. Tucked in the motel room the kind stranger—Laredo—had procured. White walls. Western-themed art. Beige carpet and a floral spread atop a comfortable bed.

A few more blinks followed by deep breaths brought her fully awake.

Lark fitfully cried.

"Coming, sweetie…" Wincing from the purple bruises along her back and rib cage, Robin went to the portable crib the motel had provided, lifting her six-month-old into her arms for a comforting squeeze. "Shh… It's okay. Mommy's here. Let's get you fed."

Robin hugged Lark with one arm, then used her free hand to bunch the pillows. Back in the bed with the comfy mound of pillows behind her, she lifted her T-shirt, welcoming the instant relief of her milk flowing when the baby hungrily latched on.

The room was silent save for Lark's soft moans and grunts.

Robin closed her eyes, trying to relax. But it was hard. She had to keep reminding herself that the worst was behind her. That every passing car on the highway wasn't en route to find her. The sheriff not only didn't know who she was but didn't care.

Deep breaths, she reminded herself.

In and out.

Nice and slow.

In and—

A knock on the room's door startled her, which in turn interrupted Lark's breakfast. A fact that the baby protested with an angry wail. Part of Robin was afraid to open the door—terrified of who may lurk behind it. Another part of her was tired of running. Of being afraid. That woman covered herself for modesty, clung to her crying baby, then peered through the door's peephole.

When she saw Laredo, a rush of air vacated her lungs.

Just as she remembered from their previous encounter, he was tall and solid and under ordinary circumstances, just the right sort of man she may have turned to for a protector. But she was no longer that woman and she certainly didn't have the luxury of trusting anyone other than herself.

Her only goal was to leave this town ASAP.

The best thing Laredo had going for him was his ability to assist her with that short-term need.

Upon opening the door, she stepped back to grant him entrance. “Come on in. I’m not quite ready, and it’s chilly.”

“Thanks.” For a moment, he froze as if not sure how to react to the sight of a mother breastfeeding her child—no matter how discreetly. “Um, want me to come back in a few?”

“No. She’s almost done.”

“Great.” With a nice recovery, he wagged a paper sack and a drink holder carrying two divine-smelling coffees. “Two weeks ago a new coffee shop opened down the road. Clovis specializes in the sort of gourmet doughnuts you might see in a big city. What she doesn’t get is that around here glazed or a nice chocolate Long John suit most folks just fine. Anyway, sorry about this monstrosity of a frosted extravaganza—” he handed her the bag “—but I was running late, and this was the simplest of all she had left. Well, aside from the bacon variety, which I have to admit sounds too scary to even try.”

“You always talk this much?”

He chuckled. “No. But you’re a breath of fresh air. Most of the women around here are what I can only describe as hungry. They see a new man and pounce. The smart thing to do would be introducing them to one of my single SEAL friends. Jed would do. I’ll give him a long overdue call.” He shoved his hands in his jeans pockets. “At first, the attention was flattering. But then it got old. I moved up here for solitude. Sadly, every woman in town seems to have her own agenda, none of which jibe with mine.”

Robin cleared her throat. “If you don’t mind my asking, what exactly is your agenda?” Her baby was still hungry and rooted at Robin’s covered breasts.

He removed his hat, pressing it to his chest before nodding to the nearest of the two chairs flanking a small, window-front table. “Mind if I have a seat?”

“Not at all.”

“My agenda…” He took one of the coffees before sitting. “Now there’s a loaded question. The simplest answer? I’m here trying to homestead but having a devil of a time. Most folks think I’m a bit off my rocker. Others don’t have a problem with calling me flat-out crazy.”

“Are you? Crazy?” While juggling the baby, she managed to take the second coffee. Her first sip was sheer bliss—cream and lots of sugar. “This is great by the way. Thanks.”

“You like it?”

“Love it. Lucky guess on how I take it.”

He waved his hat. “Wish I could take the credit. Clovis—owner and barista—says that’s the local favorite for women around your age.”

“My age, huh?” She’d meant the question as a lighthearted jab, but he wasn’t laughing, and neither was she. Ducking back behind her coffee, she wished he’d make more small talk. When he didn’t, because emotional and physical abuse had taught her to cover awkward silences with polite chatter, she said, “I really do appreciate your help. Is the mechanic’s shop far?”

“Nah. Just a hop and skip down the road. If it wasn’t for the baby and your luggage and the lack of a sidewalk, I suppose it wouldn’t make a bad walk.” He rose, taking his coffee, but leaving her with the doughnut. “Soon as you’re ready, I’ll be waiting out in my truck.” He hitched his thumb toward the motel’s lot. “Take your time. I need to make a couple calls and answer emails.”

“Thanks.”

"No worries." He'd said that last part with one foot already out the door. Once he closed it behind him, she shivered. But not because of the temperature. It had been so long since she'd been around anyone besides her husband or his family. Her isolation had been crippling. To now not only speak to another man but be alone with him in a motel room was frightening. She didn't feel the slightest hint of danger from Laredo, but the monster from whom she'd escaped.

Robin finished feeding her fussy baby, then made quick work of packing the room, grabbing the few items she'd taken from her bags before dressing, smoothing her hair into a ponytail and brushing her teeth.

A sliver of golden sunlight filtered through a part in the curtains. From her crib, Lark clucked and cooed.

"Listen to you, my little chicken." Robin scooped her from the crib. "Do you like the sun?" She kissed the baby's chubby cheek. "Me, too."

As she forced a few deep breaths, hugging her baby close, tears stung Robin's eyes. *I'm free. I'm actually free.* And it felt surreal. As dazzling as that sliver of sun.

Her freedom transformed her spirit into one of the dust motes dancing through the air.

She shivered again.

This time from the relief of not waking up to fear for what her day might hold, but anticipation. Her tires would soon be fixed, and she and Lark would be back on the road. With each mile, they'd grow safer and safer.

As for the possibility of the new monster chasing them?

She bravely refused to give that fear life.

For now, all that mattered was this day. This moment when all was well, and her baby shimmered in sunbeams.

After eating the doughnut that was absurdly over-decorated with mini Reese's Peanut Butter Cups and chocolate chips, Robin kissed Lark once more before changing her diaper. She next used a warm, wet cloth to give her a bath, then rubbed her tiny limbs in pink lotion. Upon being dressed in a fresh pink onesie, Lark smelled as good as she looked.

After settling the baby into her carrier, along with a pink teething ring, Robin fastened the safety straps. She next made quick work of repacking the baby's supplies.

With the room clear, her satchel and diaper bags slung over her shoulders, aggravating the bruises on her back and ribs with each step, Robin left Lark's carrier near the table while she opened the door on a swirling light fog. In spots, the sun was doing its best to punch through, but the eerie desert landscape might as well have been another planet.

"Let me help," Laredo said, already out of his truck.

"Thanks."

He took her two bags, leaving Robin free to return for Lark. "Hope you don't mind," he said, "but I grabbed the base from your baby's carrier out of your car. I know we're only going a short way but figured it's always best to err on the side of caution."

"True. Thanks."

He opened the passenger-side door. "Let me help. It's a high reach." Taking the baby's carrier, he soon had it snapped into the base. "All set."

"How do you know so much about baby equipment? It took me a few weeks to perfect that move."

"Long story with no good answer."

Okay… Could he be more cryptic? Didn't matter. After about ten minutes, they'd never see each other again.

Besides, she had her own secrets.

He was entitled to his.

After shutting the door on Lark, he took the satchel and diaper bag, placing them in the truck's bed before rounding to the open driver's-side door. "You're next."

She understood that Lark's safety seat made the awkward seating arrangement a necessity. Maybe if she wasn't so emotionally exhausted, it wouldn't be any big deal—squeezing herself into the cramped truck cab, then holding her breath when Laredo climbed in alongside her.

The thin denim of her jeans didn't block the rising heat between their pressed thighs. The sensation proved as unnerving as it was oddly comforting. This man had been saving her since the moment they'd met, and here he was, bright and early, charging to her rescue once again.

"Sorry about the tight squeeze."

"It's okay."

He took a worn leather cowboy hat from the truck's dusty dash, then slapped it on his head. "We don't have far."

They could have traveled five hundred feet but being this close to the kind stranger felt more like a journey of a thousand miles. Something about him made her hot and confused. The sooner she and Lark got on their way, the better.

They were headed for Eureka Springs, Arkansas, where her grandparents lived. Part of her felt guilty for exposing them to potential danger should trouble find her there. But her grandmother assured her the tight-knit community knew how to look after one of their own.

As Laredo promised, they didn't have far to travel.

A few minutes later, they'd reached the mechanic's shop that looked like it had once been a gas station. Abandoned cars with windshields coated in dust had been parked alongside newer models Robin assumed were in line for service.

Laredo parked his truck in front of a bench made of rusty tire rims topped by a bright yellow cushion.

"I swear," he said after turning off the truck's engine, "Jimmy's fiancée has made it her life's mission to clean this place up. I don't see it happening but bless her heart for trying."

Robin smiled at the sight of hanging flowerpots overflowing with red petunias. A well-swept path led through mounds of scrap metal toward the shop's door, which had been decorated with an ivy-wrapped wreath and dangling weathered wood sign that read, *HOWDY NEIGHBORS*. "I think it's sweet she cares."

He grunted before opening the passenger door to take Lark from her seat. He seemed like a natural with her. Could he have had a child of his own? Or was she reading more into it than there was? Probably the latter.

Without incident, he handed over her daughter.

The sun had burned off nearly all the fog, and now beat with surprising intensity for this early in the morning. She wore a pale blue short-sleeved blouse and Laredo had rolled the sleeves on his heavy tan work shirt. His forearms were muscular and bronzed. Golden hairs glinted in the sun. When he brushed against her, the moment may have been brief, but the unexpected bolt of awareness for him as a man and her as a woman was not only unfamiliar, but unwelcome.

She drew back as swiftly as he did.

Good to see they were on the same page.

He left her to jog ahead, opening the shop's door for her.

Inside the dim office that smelled of new tires and old 10W-40, a man with hair redder than the petunias sat behind a seventies-era gray metal desk, hunched over, resting his forehead against his palms.

"Jimmy?" Laredo asked. "You okay?"

With a start, the twentysomething mechanic with freckles that matched his hair glanced up. "Hey. I'm assuming you're here about the tires?"

"Yes." Robin stepped forward. "Sorry to be a bother, but I really need to get back on the road. Do you have the tires in stock?"

He sighed. "'Fraid not. In fact, I just got off the phone with my usual delivery service out of Grand Junction. Their truck broke an axle. They're waiting for a replacement out of Denver."

"Can't they use another?" Robin asked. The longer she stayed in the same place, the greater the risk of being caught.

"I wish." Sighing, the shop owner shook his head. "I've got six jobs ahead of yours and a fiancée who thinks my only job should be helping her plan our wedding. Every one of those vehicles need parts that are on that truck. Even worse, I need the money from those customers to make the final payment on the reception hall—Sally doesn't know that last part."

"I'm sure they'll fix the truck soon."

"How far is it?" Robin asked. "To Grand Junction?"

"Four hours." Laredo drummed his fingers atop a tall laminated counter. "Jimmy, would it help if I picked up the parts for you?"

"Thanks, but it's still early. I'd hate for you to go all that way only to have them call and say they figured out a fix."

"Roger that." Laredo turned to Robin. "Look, I didn't expect to be in town this long. I guess that leaves two options. Either you and the baby camp out here, or you could tag along with me to the feed store, then pick up my new goats."

"Thanks, but I'll—" Robin had been on the verge of telling Laredo she'd wait at the shop as long as it took to get new tires, but then she got a nasty shock when a flash outside caused her to glance beyond the office's large picture window.

Pulling into the lot was an SUV marked *SHERIFF*.

Her pulse raced nearly as hard as it had the previous day when that man had taken her car and baby. Had the sheriff found out what she'd done? Was he here to arrest her?

She gripped her baby tighter. "Um, Laredo, I think it might be fun for Lark if we tag along. She's never seen a goat."

"I've got your cell number." Jimmy waved them on their way. "You two get going. It's time for Kyle's regular oil change. At least that's something I can do without new parts."

*Yes*. Robin willed her heart to slow. Let's go *now*.

"Sounds like a plan." Laredo already stood at the office door, holding it open for her. "Catch you later, Jimmy."

The phone rang. Jimmy waved again before answering.

"I thought that was your ride," Kyle said. "Ma'am, did Jimmy get you hooked up with your new tires?"

"Not yet." Robin prayed the sheriff would enter the shop through the open garage doors. Instead, he stood between her and Laredo's truck. She shuffled past. "Excuse me. I need to change my baby's diaper."

"Sure." He tipped his uniform hat. "Nice seeing you again. Hope you get back on your way soon."

Robin held her breath until safely reaching the truck.

Lark's diaper was fine.

Robin's pounding heart told another story. Until her tires were replaced, she had a new primary goal—staying as far from the sheriff as possible.

# *Chapter 3*

"That gal's as skittish as a day-old colt."

"Worse." Laredo shared a laugh with Kyle.

What he didn't share were his suspicions that Mary was hiding from something. Most likely causes? An abusive ex. Trouble with the law. Evading debt. There were any number of reasons that could explain her standoffish behavior. What Laredo couldn't explain was why he felt protective toward a woman and baby he barely knew.

"What's the story on her tires? I figured a car as common as hers wouldn't be a tough fit."

"It's not." Laredo explained the delivery truck issue.

"Ah… The joys of small-town living. Might be faster to order from Amazon."

"True." Laredo removed his hat, using it to fan the day's rising heat from his face. With the morning fog burned off, endless blue sky crowned the day. If it hadn't been for the tumbleweed at his feet and swaying brown grasses on the horizon, he might have been back at sea. Sometimes he missed aspects of his former life. The camaraderie. The intensity. His full eyesight. "Hopefully, Jimmy will get the tires sorted out soon."

"Agreed. Need me to take the gal and her baby off your hands? She's welcome to hang out at the station. The break room's set up for overnights. I've got extra deputies hired for Wing-Ding Days."

Laredo winced. "Is it that time of year again already?"

"'Fraid so, my friend." Kyle laughed, landing a pat to his shoulder. "Chin up. It'll be fun. It brings a truckload of cash into local businesses. Sarah says the motel is already booked and Lulu's making extra pies to sell at the arts and crafts show. The mayor's expecting a few thousand folks."

Laredo snorted on the way to his truck. With a backhanded wave, he added, "That's my cue to stay out at my place till next week."

"Party pooper!" Kyle shouted.

After climbing behind the wheel, Laredo backtracked. "Forgot the dirty diaper. Hand it to me, and I'll toss it in Jimmy's dumpster."

"Oh—" She looked down, fastening the baby's safety harness. "False alarm."

Was it? Or had she invented the diversion to avoid Kyle?

Keeping his suspicions to himself, he started the engine, backing up before heading through more traffic than he'd seen since leaving San Diego.

"Is there something going on in town?"

"Wing-Ding Days." He groaned when it took a few minutes' wait to make a simple left into the feed store lot.

"Come again?" She flashed what he suspected was her first genuine smile since they'd met. "That sounds odd."

"It is." He steered through the temporary clearing. "The way I heard it explained is that the annual chicken races are in celebration of the town's founder who owned the state's first chicken farm. Sadly, they all died—George Whitlock and his fowl—in an epic 1913 blizzard. Can you believe they had thirty-eight inches of snow? Denver had forty-five."

*"Wow."*

"I know, right?" He parked in front of the store.

"But how did that tragedy result in chicken racing? And how does one even go about racing chickens?"

Laredo laughed. "No clue on both counts. Don't forget funnel cakes, corn dogs and carnival rides. This time tomorrow, the whole town will be a madhouse. Kyle even hired extra help."

"Thankfully, I should be long gone by then."

"Lucky you. But I'll be fine. My place is a good hour outside of town."

She nodded and smiled.

Something about the way the sun shone through the window, backlighting her hair, squeezed his chest. She was impossibly pretty. And smelled good—clean and soapy. Like the wholesome new mom from a baby shampoo commercial. It was a struggle to force himself to remember she wasn't selling hair care products, but a lie.

Something about her didn't ring true.

"Hang tight," he said, hating the war inside himself. For the few more hours he'd be with her, he made the conscious decision to become the proverbial ostrich sticking his head in the sand. "I need to grab a couple bags of feed for my chickens, then we'll pick up the goats."

"Sounds fun." Another genuine smile warmed him in places where it had been years since he'd last seen light. "I haven't pet a goat in forever. Had to be back when I was little, and my folks took me to the county fair."

"You and Lark's father never took her?" *Go in the store, Laredo.* Don't be an idiot by getting any more involved with a woman who not only has something to hide but is leaving town in a few hours.

"He, um, didn't care for things like that."

*Go inside, stupid.* Why was he short on breath? "Are you still with him?"

She shook her head. Was it his imagination, or had the color left her face as if his question had been the plug on an emotional drain?

"Never mind. None of my business."

"It's okay," she said. "No. We're no longer married."

"Oh." Shoving his hands into his pockets, he nodded. "Well, I'm sorry to hear that." *No, you're not.* "Let me grab the feed, then we'll show Lark her first goat."

Her smile was faint, but the light behind Mary's eyes held an emotion on which he couldn't quite get an accurate read. Maybe hope?

He caught her stare and in that frozen moment found a kindred spirit. Another soul who was a little lost. Alone. The notion was as disconcerting as it was ludicrous.

"Right." He marked the official end of the conversation, the moment, the crazy yearning for something he hadn't realized he'd been missing, with a nod. "I'm gonna get that feed."

Only after trudging ten yards into the store did Laredo realize he still hadn't breathed.

The sooner *Mary* left town, the better.

* * *

"Aren't you an itty-bitty slice of sweet potato pie?" The woman who'd introduced herself as Augusta Wren jiggled Lark's pink-covered foot. She held out her arms. "I can't remember the last time I got to hold a baby. Would you mind?"

"Um, I guess that would be okay. Should we sit down?"

They backed onto old-fashioned white metal gliders, then Robin passed the baby to her new friend. Augusta seemed like a nice-enough lady. Tall, she wore khaki shorts and an orange-toned tie-dyed T-shirt. A huge, flowery floppy hat shaded her face from the harsh sun. Cowboy boots protected her legs and feet from ground hazards. She and her husband ran a goat farm, and while Laredo and her husband, Ned, loaded his new herd, Robin had chatted with Laredo's neighbor on their shady back porch that was an oasis of green in the otherwise brown landscape.

A fountain made from an assortment of stacked metal parts merrily tinkled, sending an occasional cool spray riding the soft breeze.

Hanging ferns and spider plants mingled with the tops of potted palms and fig trees. Colorful glazed Mexican pottery bowls had been filled with H2O, providing homes for water hyacinth and lettuce.

"This is beautiful," Robin said with genuine awe. She'd always envied people born with green thumbs.

"Thanks. It's a lot of work, but a labor of love. Ned and I enjoy our exotic paradise right here in the middle of our dust farm." She smiled Robin's way before returning her attention to making goofy faces at giggly Lark. "How long have you known Laredo?"

"Gosh…" Robin had to stop and think. "You know, I don't think it's even been twenty-four hours." She gave the CliffsNotes version of her carjacking and Jimmy's woes with the delivery truck. "As soon as my tires are replaced, I'll be on my way."

"How awful. We've never had anything like that happen in town—and I should know. Been here all my life."

"It's okay." Robin looked to her clasped hands on her lap. "I mean, it's not, but everything worked out fine. Thank goodness Lark didn't get hurt."

"Amen." The older woman kissed Lark's cheek. "Are you thirsty? I've got tea or could make lemonade. It's from a mix, but still tasty on a barn burner of a day like this."

"Thank you, but it's probably almost time for us to go."

"Probably so. But let me know if you change your mind. Your hero has always been a favorite of mine."

*My hero.*

That's exactly what Laredo had turned out to be. How would Robin ever repay his many kindnesses? Her ex had done nothing for free. Payment in one form or another was always expected. The sobering thought shocked her back to reality as effectively as a glass of ice water sloshed in her face. As much as she may be enjoying this time with Augusta, Robin had to get back on the road. Soon. The farther she got from the mess she'd left in California, the better.

Augusta said, "Ned told me that Laredo's partially blind. That's why he had to leave the Navy. And why he never drives at night."

But he did drive in the dark last night—*for me.*

"Ned was a Marine. I sometimes envy how military

men seem to belong to a brotherhood. I suppose it's the same for women who've served."

"Probably. My grandfather was in Vietnam. He didn't speak of it much, but then one of the guys he'd fought with came to town. The two hung out in Grandpa's office, talking for hours. I remember hearing a lot of laughs—even some crying."

"That was a terrible time." Augusta focused her stare on the horizon. "Ned broke his leg in two places during a training exercise and never had to go. I still feel guilty about being relieved when I heard the news. We had so many friends who died." The woman seemed to have retreated inside herself, but then swiped tears from her eyes and forced a smile. "Gracious, how did we get turned around to such a deep topic? Should we grab a few smiles by seeing how our men are getting along down at the barn?"

"Sounds good." Robin could use a smile. She'd seen more than enough sadness in her life. "Let me take Lark. She weighs more than you'd think after carrying her for a while."

Augusta laughed, holding up the infant to Robin's waiting arms. Taking the baby hurt her many bruises, but she soldiered through.

The two walked the hundred yards to the barn in silence save for the sounds of their feet crunching the winding, pea gravel path and the faint rush of a breeze caressing the valley floor. The activity worsened her pain, but she'd long since learned to compartmentalize. This hadn't been the first time Chuck beat her, but it was the last.

Laredo had built a raised wooden pen around his truck bed that currently held four goats. While the furry beasts contentedly munched hay, Laredo and Ned were out of breath, laughing.

"Now, you show up." Ned leaned against the truck, wiping his sweaty brow with his forearm.

"Those little ladies can kick." Laredo hunched over, bracing his hands on his thighs.

"My girls?" Augusta laughed. "Never. They're always well behaved." She cast Robin a conspiratorial wink.

Ned snorted. "Woman, when's the last time you carried one of your ladies to a truck?"

"Always complaining," Augusta teased. "Remind me why I married you?"

"Hmm... Was it my devastating good looks or my empty bank account? Remind me."

She kissed him with the passion of the young woman she must've been when she'd found out about his broken leg. Because the love Robin believed she'd shared with Chuck hadn't been real, she could only imagine Augusta's relief.

While the older couple canoodled, Robin shared a sideways glance with Laredo. He seemed as uncomfortable with Ned and Augusta's PDA as Robin. Had he also been burned by love?

Turning her back on the happy couple—not because she begrudged them their joy, but because she'd once wanted that sort of connection so desperately herself—Robin gravitated toward the pen holding more does and their kids.

"Look, sweetie," she said to Lark. "Those are babies like you." She knelt to pet one of the tiniest kids through the chain-link fence.

Lark kicked and gurgled with excitement, pinching her fingers toward the adorable creature.

Laredo entered the yard though the latched gate, then scooped up the furry baby, carrying it to Robin and Lark.

At first, it bleated, but then settled into Laredo's arms.

"What do you think?" Laredo crouched in front of Lark.

The baby bucked and squealed.

Laredo turned the tiny goat sideways, securing and stroking its head so Lark could safely pat the creature's soft, spotted fur.

"Is it just me," Robin said, "or if this adorable pair starred in a YouTube video, would they have five million views?"

"I was thinking more around seven..."

Their shared laugh felt as good, as innocent and pure, as Lark's blissful expression.

"Aw, aren't they the sweetest..." Augusta and her hubby strolled over arm-in-arm.

"Mary," Ned said, "I can already tell you're gonna have to buy that little gal a goat for a pet."

"Not today." With a sigh, Robin rose.

Lark screamed with displeasure, bucking and reaching for her new furry friend.

"I'm sorry, angel." Robin angled Lark's back to the kid. "Mister Laredo probably has things to do, and we need to get you to your great-grandma and grandpa."

"Where do they live?" Augusta asked while Laredo returned the kid to his or her pen.

"Arkansas. In a small town in the Ozarks called Eureka Springs. It's not easy to get to, but worth the steep and winding trip. Tons of Victorian architecture and charm."

"Sounds nice." Ned turned to Laredo. "Now that I finally talked our neighbor into learning how to care for goats, I can sneak Augusta away for a much-deserved second honeymoon. It's been too long since we've been away."

"Why would I want to go anywhere when I have everything I need right here?"

The two shared another kiss.

Talk about a couple being lucky in love. Outside of movies, based on her own experience, Robin no longer believed real love existed. Could she have been wrong?

Laredo cleared his throat. "Thanks again, Ned. Once I get the girls settled in and introduce them to Charger, I'll come back for lessons on making cheese and butter."

"Sounds like a plan."

After settling still-huffy Lark into her safety seat, Robin gave Augusta a goodbye hug. She couldn't say why, but she'd felt an instant affinity for the woman. She was sorry this would be the last time she saw her.

Laredo took it slow on the dirt road leading to his homestead. Three of the lady goats comfortably rested, but one bleated and fussed—kind of like Lark, who could hardly keep her eyes open but was determined to fight a much-needed nap.

Exhaustion also clung to Robin, but it was more of a weariness of her soul than her body.

"Do you think we should go ahead and call Jimmy?" she asked. "Just in case there's been a delivery truck miracle?"

"Good idea." He pulled his Ford to the side of the road. Though he needn't have bothered as they hadn't seen another vehicle in fifteen minutes. "Mind fishing my cell from the glove box?"

"Sure." She wiped her sweating palms on the thighs of her jeans while he made the call.

Her car *had* to be ready.

She needed to escape the feeling of wanting to belong. Augusta and Ned had seemed like the sort of people with whom you'd want to share dinner and game night—not that she'd ever indulged in such a thing, but she'd always wanted to. And Laredo was proving kind. But looks could be deceiving. No matter how tempting it may be, she couldn't afford to lower her guard.

"No, it's okay. I understand," he said into his cell. After a few minutes' small talk, he ended the call.

"Well?" she was almost afraid to ask.

"Want the standard bad news first or the really bad news?"

She groaned. "Neither."

"Not only will the delivery not be made today, but because of the festival traffic, they won't even try for tomorrow. On the bright side—they're guaranteeing they'll have your tires here by 9:00 a.m. Monday."

*"Monday?"* She pressed the heels of her hands to her forehead. "That's—"

"Three days from now." He placed the truck in Park, angling to face her. "I know this is the last thing you want to hear, but maybe after the shock of the carjacking, this is good? By Monday, you'll be well-rested and ready to get back on the road. All the festival traffic will have moved out and you shouldn't have any trouble getting to I-70."

"Oh—I prefer back roads."

"Why?" He made a face. "You'd make much better time on the Interstate. Come to think of it, why didn't you take I-30 through Arizona and New Mexico? I thought you were from southern California?"

"I never said where I was from."

"Your car has a California plate. Guess I assumed from your Disneyland bumper sticker you lived in the land of eternal sun."

She shook her head.

"Where did you live?"

"I don't want to talk about it."

"Why not? It's a simple question."

"San Francisco."

"Is that the truth?"

"Why would I lie?" She couldn't meet his accusing glare. Of course she was lying. Not by choice, but necessity. If she could tell him her entire story, she would. But unless Laredo turned her over to his buddy Kyle, that would only make him guilty, too.

He shook his head before putting the truck back into Drive. "You can stay with me for the weekend—or should I say hide with me?"

# *Chapter 4*

"Door's open," Laredo said forty minutes later with a nod toward the glorified shack he called home. The single-story adobe structure must have once had character, but decades of blowing dust had left it in need of paint and constant sweeping. Weeds poked through the wood front porch planks and a Western bluebird couple had built a nest on the sill of one of the four-paned windows. "Make yourself comfortable. I need to get the goats in the pen."

"Let me help."

"I've got it." He drummed his fingers on the wheel. Why wouldn't she go? "Head inside and get the baby out of the sun."

"What changed?" She'd clasped her hands on her lap and focused her gaze on them.

"What do you mean?"

"You haven't said a word since stopping to call Jimmy.

In the whole day I've known you—" she glanced up to flash him a faint smile "—you've rarely stopped talking."

He arched his head back and sighed. He didn't want to do this now, but since they'd be together for the next few days, he might as well put his cards on the table. "The truth? I know you're lying—about everything."

"N-not *everything*."

"Semantics. Be straight with me."

"Wish I could, but…"

From the truck bed, a goat bleated.

"Never mind." Laredo opened his door and exited the truck. He couldn't take another second of being crammed alongside a woman who lied as easily as she breathed.

Been there. Done that.

Rounding the truck, he opened the passenger side and popped the baby's carrier from the base. "Come on. I need to drive the goats down to the pen. Then I need to see about my horse, Charger. He's seemed a bit lonely, and I read online that they get along well with goats."

She seemed frozen to the truck's bench seat.

Goat unrest ran rampant.

"Correction," he said. "They probably get along well with well-mannered goats—not the rowdy bunch I presently have on my hands."

All four protested captivity with mournful bleats. Maybe he should have second-guessed not only his decision to take in Mary and her daughter, but the other four ladies in his life.

"Mary…" He ran his hand over his whisker-stubbled jaw.

"I don't want you to think bad of me." She bowed her head. "I hate myself enough. Having you hate me, too…"

"I don't hate you. I don't know you well enough to

summon that much emotion. But I'd be lying if I said I don't feel comfortable not knowing what I've gotten myself into. Taking a wild stab, I'm guessing you're on the run? Maybe from an abusive husband? Something worse? Whatever it is, let me help."

"You can't."

"How do you know if you don't ask?"

While pondering his question, she drew her lower lip into her mouth.

The goats grew rowdier.

The sun beat down on his shoulders and the baby. He held his hand over her head for shade.

"For now," he said, "let's table the topic. Get your daughter out of this heat."

Mary slid from the truck to take the baby from his arms. "I didn't lie about everything. I am going to see my grandparents. Lark is my daughter's name."

"Want a trophy?"

Tears welled in her big, brown gaze. She fairly cowered against the truck's side panel. Was she afraid of him? The notion made him instantly regret his harsh words. More than ever, he was convinced she was hiding from an abusive ex. If Laredo's assumptions were right, he could not only help her, but better secure the place in the off chance her bastard ex somehow found his wife and daughter.

"Sorry," he said. "Do me a favor and see what you can scrounge up for lunch. My doughnut wore off a while ago."

Without a word, she turned from him to enter the house.

He shut the truck's passenger door, then climbed back behind the wheel to drive the goats to their pen. Judging by Mary's instant tears and the way she'd seemed to shrink within herself, Laredo decided to give her a pass on the lies.

Didn't happen often, but once in a while they'd had a SEAL brother turn to abuse as a coping mechanism. The wives took in the victim and any children while the guys ensured it never happened again. Sometimes counseling helped. When it didn't, lives were more often than not irrevocably damaged.

He backed up to the pen's entrance—only it was really more of a yard he'd enclosed with wire fencing. It was about the size of half a football field. They'd have plenty of space to explore, plus the shade of an old cottonwood tree. Eventually, the ladies could roam free, but Ned advised letting them first get settled. Having already set out fresh hay, water and feed earlier that morning, his only remaining task was to haul the bleating beasts from the truck.

The first two went willingly, but the last two fought every brutal, dusty step, bleating and bucking until Laredo finally had all four safely in the pen.

His chestnut gelding, Charger, stood at the pasture's wooden fence appraising the scene with snorting superiority. "What's the problem, buddy?" He sauntered over to rub the chestnut's nose. "Are you thinking these rowdy goats ruin our otherwise peaceful neighborhood?"

Charger snorted.

"You're probably right."

He gave the horse an extra scoop of feed and filled his water, promising a ride in the morning.

From the barn, he hefted the chicken feed over his right shoulder, then moseyed to the coop. After dropping the bag to the ground, he used his pocket knife to slash it open, then fed the clucking ladies.

His lone rooster stood back, appraising him as if somehow finding him lacking.

"Keep it up, mister." Laredo tossed a handful of feed his way. "One of these days you'll push me too far and wind up as my Sunday supper."

Laredo lingered longer than necessary at his coop. He gave the water pan a good cleaning, then raked the fifteen-by-fifteen caged enclosure even though he'd done it the previous afternoon.

Wiping sweat from his brow with his forearm, after sweeping out the coop and filling the nesting boxes with fresh straw, it occurred to Laredo that he was stalling.

That scene with Mary had been unsettling. The worst of which was that he didn't know why. So what if the woman was lying? Odds were, she had good reason. Besides, it wasn't as if she'd be in his life beyond the next three days. Why did he care how she chose to handle her private affairs?

"Laredo!" she called out the front door. "Lunch is ready!"

Swell.

Though his stomach rumbled, he still wasn't ready to face her. Part of him felt bad for his accusatory tone. Another part was irrationally peeved about her refusal to open up to him. Which made him sound like a fourteen-year-old girl pouting to have been excluded from the day's juiciest gossip. But whatever Mary was keeping a secret, it wasn't fodder for tea, but her life.

He didn't go around spilling his innermost thoughts. Why should she?

"Ladies," he said to his flock of ten hens. "Do you think I'm overreacting?"

Judging by the increase in clucks and warbles, either they wholeheartedly agreed or wanted more feed.

"Some help you are…"

He stepped out of the pen, closed it, stashed the feed in a storage bin, then strolled across the dirt driveway leading toward the house's stubby brick walk and pitiful excuse for a yard that was more weeds than grass.

He'd just stepped onto the porch when Mary popped open the screen door.

"There you are. I was going to call you again."

"Thanks. I went ahead and fed the chickens."

"Oh." She turned to go inside. "How do the goats like their new home?"

"They seemed content enough to me. Ornery creatures damned near broke my ribs while I hauled them out of the truck."

Her gaze widened. Alarm? "Do you need to see a doctor?"

"Nah. Nothing a few Ibuprofen and a good night's sleep won't fix."

"Sure? Sometimes what feel like minor injuries at the time can turn out serious."

"Is this coming from experience?" The instant the too-personal question popped out, Laredo wanted to take it back.

Tears pooled in her eyes, but she turned her back on him before they spilled.

She crossed the smallish living room with its mismatched furniture and brown shag carpet. There was hardwood beneath. He'd been meaning to refinish the house's original mesquite floors but hadn't had time. Or the desire. He couldn't care less what the house looked like. Only now, seeing the run-down place through Mary's eyes, did he see how shabby the structure truly was.

"What smells good?" he asked, closing the screen door behind him. Maybe by pretending everything between them was normal, it would be.

"Grilled cheese and tomato soup. A nice, cool salad may have been more appropriate for this heat, but you're fresh out of greens."

"Yeah." He removed his cowboy hat, hanging it on the rack alongside the door. "My garden didn't show as much yield as I would have liked. Next summer, I need to work on my hydration system."

"I'm sure it's tough out here—keeping your plants adequately watered."

"A constant struggle."

The galley kitchen was as run-down as the rest of the place, with cabinets in need of painting and appliances and countertops older than he was. More items he planned on replacing but hadn't yet gotten around to. Since he was the only one ever here, that sort of cosmetic detail never much seemed to matter.

The baby cooed in her carrier that Mary had set alongside the table.

"Have a seat," Mary said. "I'll bring you your meal."

"Thanks, but that's not necessary. Since you cooked, I'll serve myself. I'll wash up, too."

"Let me. Really. It's the least I can do for all you've done."

Sensing this was important to her—in some small way repaying him—he forced a smile before washing his hands, then sitting at the round oak table that he typically only used while paying the monthly bills. Not only had Mary cleared his stacks of unopened mail and strewn papers, but she'd scrubbed the surface until it now glowed.

"Here you go..." She set a plate in front of him. A real glass plate—not the paper he favored. And then a soup-filled bowl. The meal did smell heavenly.

"Thanks," he said before digging in. His first bite of the cheesy sandwich left him groaning with pleasure. "Wow..."

She took the chair opposite him, starting with her soup. "It's okay?"

"Phenomenal. Although, considering my diet mainly consists of scrambled eggs, boiled eggs, and peanut butter and jelly, I'm probably not your most discerning diner."

She flashed a shy smile before ducking back to her soup. "My grandma used to make this for me. We had it a couple times a week. I used to think it was boring until I missed her. Now, every time I taste this combination, I feel like I'm back in her kitchen."

"Did she raise you?"

"Her and my grandpa. My mom died in a car accident when I was three. I'm ashamed to say it, but aside from photos, I don't remember her. Grandma's the only mother I know."

"What about your dad?" he asked after swallowing his latest bite of sandwich.

"While in the Army, he died from being too close to a suicide bomber in Iraq. I was two, but again, like my mom, have no memory of him."

"Man..." He dropped his sandwich and shook his head. "Talk about family tragedy. I'm so sorry."

She shrugged. "I can't mourn what I never knew. Plus,

I was blessed to have had grandparents who showered me with love."

"When did Lark's father come into the picture?"

She froze, but then faced him head-on. "My ex was—is—a club and music festival promoter. He was in Eureka Springs doing the preliminary legwork for a weekend country music extravaganza. Grandma and Grandpa run a boutique hotel in a refurbished bathhouse. He rented the whole place for his team. When I wasn't working as a teacher's aide, I helped with the restaurant and bar, we got to know each other in the two weeks he was there. When he returned for the festival, we, um—well, we got further acquainted. I discovered I was pregnant and he flew out from California, marrying me the next day. He took me back to his, um, San Francisco home and that was that."

"Where is he now? I'm assuming you're divorced?"

Nodding, she asked, "When do I get to quiz you?"

"I'm an open book." He popped the last bite of his sandwich into his mouth. "What do you want to know?"

"Lulu mentioned you being a Navy SEAL. What in the world drove you this far inland?"

"Fair question." Needing a sec to compose an answer that sounded neither pathetic nor too harsh, he dove into his soup. After downing half the bowl, he said, "Don't get me wrong, I'd do anything for my SEAL brothers, but sometimes that whole life got too intense. When we were away on missions, my days somehow felt amped up. Then when we got home, nothing seemed fast enough. Food didn't taste as good and music sounded as if it was missing the base. To compensate, I drank too much. My ex-wife—Carrie—was all about the eternal party. She also very much bought into the hype of the whole

Navy SEAL package. Make no mistake, we're badass, but human. When my drinking started affecting job performance, my CO put me in rehab. My counselor was big into farm therapy—which was focusing my energy on animals and plants. Go figure—I loved it. Keeping a garden and livestock alive is no joke. It might not involve playing with weapons, but for the first time in my life I felt peace. Control. I bought this property and filed for early retirement. When I surprised my wife with the news on our third anniversary, I thought she'd be excited by this new chapter. You know, a chance for us to start over away from all the distractions that threatened to tear us apart. Deep down, I believed this was our ultimate fresh start." He snorted. "Far from it. She called me a psycho loser and filed for divorce the next day. Last I heard, she'd married another SEAL and still lives in San Diego."

"Whoa..." His guest swiped silvery tears with the backs of her hands. "That's terrible."

"Oh—I failed to mention the part where she'd tricked me into marrying her by telling me she was pregnant. It killed me when I'd gotten the nursery ready and installed a car seat only to have her lose the baby. After our divorce, a mutual friend's wife told me she'd faked the whole thing."

"That's cold. Like creepy cold."

"Right?"

They finished their soup in silence.

The howling wind reminded him of the place's usual solitude and how good it felt sharing a meal with not just her, but anyone.

"Lord..." He sighed. "Sorry for dumping on you like

that. I haven't thought about that stuff in a while. Still raises my dander."

"I see why. Do you have family who helped you through?"

"Nah. Mom and Dad are in Montana. I have two older brothers up there and they both have huge families. Since joining the Navy, I've always felt like an outsider. My plan is to get this place up and running, then invite the whole crew down for a visit."

"Sounds nice." While he'd blathered on, she'd finished her meal and now stood to gather both of their dishes.

Her chubby-cheeked baby had fallen asleep.

"Let me help." He rose to lend a hand but ended up colliding with Mary in a tangle of plates and arms. His forearms, hands and entire face overheated. Something about the woman dulled his normal edge. How had he managed to find a siren in the middle of the high plains? "Excuse me."

"It's okay."

She backed away with a half smile.

Had she felt it, too? The spark of attraction that had no business being there, but for him anyway, was as undeniable as the sky being blue.

He set his plate and bowl on the counter a safe distance from where she stood at the sink.

After inserting the rubber stop over the drain, she filled the sink with warm water, adding a squirt of dishwashing liquid. "Now that your goats are safe in their new home and you avoided a trip to the ER, what do you have planned for the rest of the day?"

"I should head out to the garden. Judging by my brown squash, I think one of my irrigation hoses busted."

"Do you have any veggies to pick?"

"There are always tomatoes, zucchini and green beans."

"My grandfather has a huge garden. Grandma cans enough produce to feed half their county."

"Nice. To make this place self-sustainable, canning is something I should learn. Wish you were going to be around long enough to teach me."

"Sorry. I would, but as soon as my car's fixed…"

"Yeah…" He frowned. "I get it."

The baby woke with a few whimpers.

"Somebody missed her lunchtime," Mary said. She dried her hands on a dish towel, then plucked Lark from her carrier. "Hungry?"

While Mary patted her rump, the infant fussed all the more.

"Hungry and a wet diaper. Never a good combo." To Laredo she asked, "Where would be a good place for us to set up a temporary nursery?"

Again, he viewed his house with a critical eye. Not a single room was nice enough or clean enough for Mary and her child.

"Tell you what," he said. "Let's table the garden till it cools off outside. For now, let's make you and the munchkin a proper nest."

"What do you have in mind?"

"If you feel up to helping—after you finish feeding Lark—I think with enough sweat equity we might be able to salvage the back bedroom. I bought this place furnished and since the room was too girlie for my taste, I've been using it for storage, but I'll haul boxes to the barn if you can handle washing sheets and blankets, dusting and the like."

"Deal. Let me get Lark back to her usually smiley self, then we'll get started."

While carting his first load, Laredo couldn't remember the last time he'd felt more energized or alive. Filled with direction and purpose. All of which should make him happy.

But it didn't.

Because he had no business attaching his well-being to an admitted liar who was only biding her time till she escaped.

# Chapter 5

Robin changed Lark on the pad from her diaper bag. After a quick hand wash, she tossed a fuzzy pink receiving blanket over her shoulder, then sat on the sofa and raised her blouse, unfastening her nursing bra so her cranky angel could latch on. "There you go." She exhaled from the release of her milk's painful pressure. "That's better."

Her pulse revved when Laredo opened the screechy screen door, then stepped through. For an awkward moment, their gazes locked, but then he smiled. His forehead and cheeks glistened with sweat. His T-shirt clung to his hard chest, shoulders and biceps. His perfection made him seem not quite real. But then she'd once thought the same about her husband and look how that had turned out.

She forced herself to return his friendly gesture. "I'll help as soon as Lark's done."

"No hurry. I've hardly made a dent."

"I don't want you to think I'm trying to get out of our deal."

"Did I say you were? And anyway, it's not as if I can feed your baby."

Before she'd thought of a response, he'd turned down the hall toward the room she had yet to see. Soon enough, he emerged carrying three boxes that nearly blocked his vision. Augusta had mentioned him being partially blind. Robin wanted to ask him about it, but now didn't seem like the right time.

He nudged open the screen door and was gone as abruptly as he'd entered.

It took six more trips before Lark had eaten her fill.

Robin assembled the portable playpen Laredo had been thoughtful enough to grab from her car, along with a plethora of the other baby gear she'd packed for her escape. She'd never meant for her marriage to end the way it did, but then a lot of things in her life hadn't gone as planned.

On the bright side, without the storms, she wouldn't have found her life's greatest blessing in Lark.

"There you go," Robin said while placing her daughter in her playpen along with plenty of her favorite squeaky toys.

Upon finding herself face-to-face with her bestie stuffed whale, her daughter cooed in delight.

Robin plugged in the baby monitor's base, setting it on a bookshelf. Tucking the other half in her back pocket, she finally got to see the space that would soon be her new room. She'd expected a lackluster area as run-down and sad as the rest of the place but couldn't have been more wrong.

Sure, the pink floral wallpaper was sun-faded and the white chenille curtains and wedding ring-patterned quilt needed a good washing, but hardwood floors showed promise beneath a thick layer of dust, as did the antique walnut vanity and dresser. The white, wrought iron bed featured ornate curves and an accidental shabby chic finish.

The room's best feature? Plenty of sun and a gently whirring ceiling fan.

"What do you think?"

Pulse pounding at Laredo's sudden appearance, Robin held her hand over her heart. How long would it take for her fear to subside?

"Sorry. Didn't mean to startle you. I know it's dusty enough to form an indoor sandstorm, but once we get it cleaned out do you think it will work?"

"I think you're being silly. It's charming. And I feel guilty for you going to this much trouble for only a few days."

"It's whatever. I needed to clean it at some point. You gave me a great excuse."

"Thank you. Truly. I would have been just as comfortable on the couch."

"I'm glad to help. Now that the boxes are cleared, what's next?"

"If you'll show me where your laundry room is, let's get the bed linens started. While they're washing, we'll take down the curtains to be cleaned, give the floors and furniture a good dusting, tackle the windows, and hopefully by then we'll still be upright enough to put the sheets in the dryer, then fit them back onto the bed before collapsing."

"Just hearing that list exhausted me. Maybe this wasn't such a great idea."

"I gave you an out by offering to crash on the sofa."

He scratched his head. Stared beyond dusty windowpanes before opening his mouth, then closing it, as if searching for words that wouldn't come. "We should get started."

What was he thinking? Why had her anticipation for their shared project soured?

While filling a mop bucket, it occurred to Laredo how dangerously close he'd come to opening himself up to this woman who would soon be gone. When she'd reminded him of her offer to crash on his sofa, he'd almost admitted that he didn't just want her to crash, but to be comfortable.

To feel at home.

But this wasn't her home and never would be.

She wasn't Carrie and no matter how much he wished he could rewrite history and have another chance at starting his own family, that wouldn't happen anytime soon—if ever—either.

Every trip into town, women made no effort to hide the fact that they were available, but he'd never been interested. What about Mary drew him in? Was it her secret? The fact that she was in trouble and he used to thrive on fixing any given lousy situation?

Lord, he'd missed being needed.

With the bucket filled, he added a squirt of Murphy's Oil Soap he'd unearthed from under the sink, then grabbed a mop from the utility closet on his return to the back bedroom. The washer pleasantly chugged and he found Mary on a stepladder, singing "Itsy Bitsy Spider" to her daughter.

"...Down came the rain and washed the spider out!" Mary's voice struck him as soft and feminine yet animated enough to hold the infant's rapt interest. Lark stared in wide-eyed wonder at her mother's dancing and jazz-hand routine from atop the ladder she used to remove dingy curtains. "Out came the sun and dried up—"

"Let me help," he said mid-verse. "Makes more sense for me to start mopping on that side of the room."

"Sure." She smiled before stepping down.

Her singing had annoyed him. The grinning baby annoyed him. The degree to which he'd been drawn to both annoyed him.

He made quick work of removing the four additional sets of window coverings.

"While you're mopping," she said, "I'll rummage through your freezer for dinner ideas."

"I can eat a sandwich."

"Wouldn't you rather have a nice meal?"

*Of course.* But *nice* meals led to pleasant conversation, which would only make it that much harder to let her go. Make no mistake, she was a looker, but this wasn't about attraction but the realization of just how lonely this place was. He'd never planned to live here alone. Carrie was supposed to have been part of the homesteading package. Now that she wasn't, he found himself dreading the long nights.

The time when his limited vision made him feel vulnerable—a state in which he'd never been and deeply resented.

"Laredo? Dinner?"

"Doesn't matter."

"Did I do something wrong?" She lifted Lark's carrier from the floor.

*Hell, yes. You're here and Carrie isn't. Which serves as a nasty reminder of how pissed I still am.* But that didn't give him the right to take out his anger on Mary. "No. I appreciate your help. Knock yourself out on any meal you'd like."

"I will. Thanks."

Laredo didn't look at her because he couldn't. His mood was too low. He'd started the project with a sense of anticipation and hope. He now realized the downside of prettying up a room for this woman and her child. No sooner than the job was completed, so would their time be with him.

Done with the curtains, he cleared the floor and refocused his attention on the task at hand. He was only a quarter of the way finished when the water had turned dirty enough that he needed to change it.

He slung the brown water off the back porch, then returned to the kitchen sink to refill it.

Still feeling bad about how he'd snipped at Mary, when he found her at the counter, chopping carrots, he asked, "What did you unearth from the freezer?"

"I found a chuck roast. It's defrosting in the microwave. Since we have plenty of time for it to simmer and lots of root veggies, I thought it would make a good stew."

He nodded. "Love stew. Haven't had it in a while. Need help?"

"No, thank you."

"Okay, then…" With the bucket refilled, he added soap and turned for the bedroom. He took ownership of the awkwardness between them. There'd been nothing overtly cross—more of a general bad vibe. Her posture had once again seemed defeated with her shoulders slumped and voice meek. The fact made him turn back. "In case I haven't mentioned it before—I appreciate your help. I can't remember the last time I've had company and I forget my manners. Sorry."

She beamed. "You have nothing to apologize for. If anything, I'm sorry for Lark and I taking over your home. We'll be gone soon, but if you'd rather we return to the motel, I can—"

"No, no. That's not what I meant." Setting the bucket on the floor, he bowed his head. "Might sound corny, but I'm glad you're here. I'm enjoying the company."

"Really?" As if shocked by his admission, her eyebrows rose, but only for an instant before she resumed chopping.

"At first, I wasn't sure, but it feels good to switch up my routine."

"I know what you mean. When I was with—well, with my ex—I was strictly a stay-at-home mom, but I used to be a teacher's assistant. I always planned to go to college and become a real teacher, but life has a way of getting in the way of plans." She set aside the completed carrots to cube already-peeled potatoes.

"Don't I know it," he said with a harsh laugh.

"I enjoyed my job, though. It was in a special education classroom, working with kids who really tugged at my heartstrings—not that they all don't, but these children glowed when learning a new letter of the alphabet or completing physical therapy. The other three assistants and the teacher and students and I formed a sweet family. I didn't realize how much I enjoyed the job till I no longer had it."

"What made you quit?"

"My pregnancy took a bad turn. My blood pressure spiked and I had to take early leave. Once Lark was born, my ex didn't want me to go back, so I didn't."

"I don't mean to pry, but what happened?"

"Nothing good." She brought the knife down extra hard on the last potato.

Would he ever learn the extent to which she'd been abused? Given they'd only be together a short while longer, probably not.

"Guess I should get back to the bedroom floor," he said.

"I've still got onions to chop."

Despite the fact that they both had tasks to complete, they stood frozen, staring. While he was fighting confusion laced with an unidentifiable something else, his breath caught in his throat. What was it about this woman that made him want to hold her in his arms and never let go? She was a stranger, yet what if she stayed? What if they got to know each other more?

He shook his head. Lunacy. "I'm gonna go finish that floor."

"Onions…"

Nodding, he picked up the bucket. He started to leave the kitchen, but then turned back to her and smiled. "I'm excited to try your stew."

"Thank you."

Before he made an even bigger fool of himself, he hightailed it for the back bedroom. Whatever he felt for the woman not only wasn't good, but downright dangerous for his new and improved simplified way of life. He didn't need a fancy meal, but a can of pork and beans. He didn't need a fancy house, but a roof over his head.

In the safety of the dimly lit hall, he froze. Closed

his eyes. Unexpected warmth and well-being spread through him like a sunbeam punching through clouds on a stormy day.

No—he didn't need any of what Mary offered. But deep down in long-buried places he'd damn sure rather forget, he sure did like her and her cooking and companionship for however briefly she'd transform his house into a home.

With Laredo out of the cramped kitchen, Robin could once again breathe. He was a large man—tall with broad shoulders and a barrel chest. But unlike her husband, Laredo didn't frighten her. More like fascinated her. The way she'd felt as a child when staring into elaborate storefront windows during the bustling holiday season.

"Is Mommy crazy?" she asked her gurgling baby.

Lark stopped mauling a stuffed rabbit ear long enough to grin from her portable playpen.

"Did you just say yes?" she teased, rinsing her hands before tickling her daughter's ribs.

Giggles ensued, flooding Robin with the sort of well-being she hadn't felt since leaving her grandparents' home. For this moment in time, encapsulated on this sweet little homestead, life was good. If only she could capture the moment—Lark's infectious giggles, the lightness in Robin's heart—storing it for later use during inevitable dark times.

The dryer buzzed.

"Time for Mommy to quit playing and get to work."

*"Grrrgffft!"*

Robin couldn't stop smiling while giving Lark's chubby tummy one more pat. "Is that your not-so-subtle version of telling me you agree?"

Robin folded the still-warm sheets and pillowcases, breathing in the fresh scent. She transferred the quilt from the washer to the dryer, then started a fresh washer load with curtains, setting it on the gentle cycle.

She was on her way to finish the stew when she heard Laredo's cell ring. It hadn't been her intention to eavesdrop, but it was kind of hard not to listen when he was in the next room.

"...You know how I feel about crowds."

Silence.

"How would my story motivate anyone?"

Another long pause.

A deep sigh.

"I'll do it, but you owe me...Whatever. When it's time to Rototill my garden, you're the first guy I'm calling." After more grumbling, Laredo ended the call.

*What was that about?* Robin turned for the kitchen.

"I know you're out there." Mop in hand, he appeared at the open bedroom door.

"I didn't mean to listen... But I was here doing laundry and..."

"I get it. It's a small house. No need to explain."

"If you don't mind my asking, who was that and why do you suddenly seem tense?"

"Kyle."

"Oh." Was it possible to feel the color drain from your cheeks? The less she heard about the sheriff, the better. "I-is there some kind of trouble?"

"No." His gaze narrowed. "Are you expecting any?"

"Not at all. But you do seem upset."

"I am." He slammed the heel of his palm against the nearest wall. "The festival always has a row of local merchants and artisans. The recruitment officer from Grand

Junction usually sets up a booth, but his wife is in labor. Kyle asked me to fill in. I guess it's already assembled, but they need someone to man the thing."

"You used to be a SEAL. I would think guys considering serving would get a kick out of talking to you."

He shrugged.

"Hope this isn't too personal, but Augusta told me about your vision."

Hands on his hips, he glanced up, then down. "She has a big mouth."

"She didn't say anything bad—just that you had trouble seeing at night. Which made me feel awful about you having to drive all this way the night we met."

"It's whatever. I deal."

"Obviously. But…"

"I'm helping Kyle, but not happy about it. Wanna tag along? At least there's good food and music."

"Will, um…Kyle be there? In the booth? With you?"

"No. And don't you think it's about time you come clean about why you're skittish around the guy?"

"Long story. Very boring."

"Uh-huh…" He returned to mopping.

She finished the stew.

The rest of the afternoon was a blur of dragging the mattress outside for airing and keeping the washer and dryer humming.

When the back bedroom was declared officially finished, Robin couldn't remember the last time she'd been more physically exhausted—but in a great way. In the light of the setting sun, the antique furniture and wood floors glowed. The gauzy curtains danced in the light breeze whispering through open screened windows.

"We did good," Laredo said. "You're a hard worker."

"So are you. Thank you. I hate that you went to all

this trouble when we're not staying that long." She held Lark on her hip and gave her a light jiggle.

"It needed a good cleaning. The whole house does. Out here on my own, guess I've always felt my time is better spent tending my animals and garden. Speaking of which... Want to help make sure everyone's tucked in for the night?"

"I'd love to." She looked to Lark. "Sound fun?"

The baby gurgled.

As they exited the front door, the whole house smelled of the slow-simmering stew. Robin's stomach growled.

Her host took his cowboy hat from a wall peg, slapping it on his head for their walk before tugging the door shut behind them.

Outside, the vast open sky was awash in pale orange, red and lavender. Lengthening shadows banished the day's heat, making the temperature cool and pleasant. The earlier breeze had stilled. The earth having exhaled in relief at the closing of the day.

"I see why you like it here," she said, holding Lark while he filled the chickens' water container. "It's enchanted."

The clucking hens mesmerized her wide-eyed daughter, who lunged toward the creatures, pinching her fingers in the universal infant sign for *"Gimme!"*

"It's okay..." He cast a slow and easy grin over his shoulder. "Wouldn't go quite so far as to call it enchanted. I'd reserve that title for the Alps. Maldives. Bali."

"You've been to all of those places?"

"Yeah—but usually with a bunch of other SEALs. I mean, the scenery is everything you'd imagine from travel brochures, but without a special someone to experience it with, the trips weren't what they could have been."

"Did you and your ex travel?"

"Sure. We did Maui for our honeymoon. An Alaskan cruise. I guess at the word *enchanted*, my mind goes to Disney-type perfection and this run-down old place *ain't* it."

"But it could be..." She spun in a circle, holding out her daughter while making silly sounds. "All you need is some paint. A few flower boxes and maybe make walking paths lined with rocks. If you really wanted to go crazy, the house and chicken coop would look darling with shutters. Maybe plant a few more indigenous trees."

"Uh-huh." He removed his cowboy hat to wipe sweat from his brow. "Woman, you're exhausting me just thinking about all that work. Lark," he said to her baby girl, "you wanna visit the goats?"

*"Pffftgggloo!"*

Laughing, he said, "I'll take that as a yes. Mind if I hold her?" He brushed his hands on the thighs of his jeans. "My paws aren't too dirty."

"Your *paws* look fine." She handed over Lark who promptly grabbed for Laredo's hat to gum the brim.

"Hey..." He tried reclaiming it, but each time he tugged it free she cried. "You win, angel. Guess it's yours now."

The sight of great big Laredo holding her itty-bitty daughter made fireflies take flight in Robin's stomach. This was how she'd always imagined having a family would be.

Instead, her old life had been a nightmare.

If she didn't stay clear of Kyle, he would make her present even worse.

# *Chapter 6*

To calm her runaway pulse, Robin forced a deep breath, slowly exhaling.

"You okay?" Laredo asked in front of the goat pen's gate.

"Sure. Just tired." She flashed a smile.

He nodded, petting the goat that came running up.

Lark giggled when the rest of the herd surrounded them, bleating for their share of attention.

"Mind getting them a few scoops of grain?" Laredo asked. "We're getting attacked over here."

"I'm on it." She was happy for the distraction.

The sight of him with her daughter made her wistful for the kind of happy ending her actions ensured she'd never have. Her only hope for a normal life was to get to her grandparents and pray they'd be able and willing to hide her from the law.

Northern Arkansas was still fairly desolate with a

lot of places to get permanently lost. Her grandfather's hunting cabin being one of them.

She opened the grain bin and was treated to the sweet smell of feed and sound of hungry nannies who now rushed the wood trough Laredo had built inside their pen.

"That should do it," he said after she'd added the third scoop. "Mind watering, too? I'm selfishly enjoying hanging out with your little one. Can't remember the last time I've held a munchkin."

*Swoon.*

After placing the lid securely on the feed bin, Robin filled the water trough with the nearby hose. Finished, she leaned against the wood fence, drinking in the view.

Dazzling sunset—check.

Adorable farm animals—check.

Gorgeous, hardworking, kind man admitting he enjoyed spending time with her baby—check, check.

Whoever was lucky enough to catch Laredo would be a happy woman for life.

"Seen enough?" he asked her daughter.

She kicked and grinned.

"Okay, we'll visit a smidge longer, but then we need to let the mamas rest. They're going to be having babies, and that's how we get milk."

"How does that whole process work?" Mary asked.

"I'm no expert, but according to Ned, once these ladies have their kids, I set up a schedule where I can either milk once or twice a day. I'm thinking once sounds saner, so I separate the kids from the nannies for twelve hours, then milk the nannies, then let the babies do the afternoon milking."

"Sounds reasonable. Are you just wanting the goat milk, or are you going to make cheese?"

"I'd love cheese. But I'm going to need more lessons." Since Lark rested her cheek against his shoulder, he inched toward the gate. "My eventual goal is to be entirely self-sufficient. Wind and solar power. Plenty of livestock. Great garden. The works."

"Sounds tough—but amazing. I admire your drive."

"Thanks. I appreciate that—a lot. My ex thought the whole setup was more than a few cukes shy of a bushel."

"We might have had a family business in the hotel, but I basically grew up in the country. We only had chickens and a garden, but we knew homesteaders who were self-reliant. My grandparents viewed it as an art. It's quite a balance—like running your own country."

"Now you've got me worried I can't handle it."

"You'll do fine—assuming you don't catch some mystery disease from your dirty house."

"Hey! That's not nice." His laugh told her he knew she'd been joking. Sort of.

"What's not nice is the layer of gunk I scrubbed from your kitchen sink."

"Sorry about that, *Mom*."

She couldn't resist sticking out her tongue.

He made a grab for it, but since she wasn't carrying a baby, Robin easily darted from his reach.

Both were laughing and short of breath by the time they'd reached the porch.

In the way only babies seemed to do, Lark had fallen asleep.

"How did that happen?" he asked, staring in wonder while cupping the crown of her head.

"No clue. Can you imagine how much drug companies could charge for a product that brought on an instant nap?"

He made a face. "Pretty sure they already have them, but we wouldn't be as cute after taking them or wake without a headache."

"True."

"Hungry?" she asked inside.

"Very. Is your stew done?"

"Should be. If you wouldn't mind settling Lark into her playpen, I'll check on dinner."

"Deal."

They both soon finished their tasks and minutes later sat at the kitchen table before steaming bowls of stew. Outside, the day's sun was just a memory painted by vibrant orange and violet streaks across the vast open sky.

The copper-domed light hanging from the kitchen ceiling bathed them in its warm golden glow, creating a cozy atmosphere that warmed her far more than the hearty meal. Cocooned in this remote corner of the world, she and her new friend might as well be on another planet. Considering her situation, a good thing.

"About tomorrow," he said from in front of the stove where he helped himself to a second serving. "I was thinking… My shift at the recruitment booth ends at two. If you want to tag along, once I'm done, we could check out the festival. Neither of us are big on crowds, but I do love a funnel cake."

A wistful smile tugged the corners of her lips. "Me, too…"

"But?"

"I didn't say anything else."

"But you were going to…"

She opened her mouth to protest, but then closed it and nodded.

"You want to know if we'll see Kyle?"

Another nod.

"I can't promise we won't, but as busy as he'll be coordinating his extra help, I'm pretty sure catching you will be the last thing on his mind."

She clasped her hands so tightly on her lap that her nails dug into her palms.

"Want more stew?" He set his bowl on the table, then nodded toward the cast iron pot.

"No, thank you."

"Ever going to tell me why you think Kyle wants to arrest you?"

"No." *But my silence is for your own protection.*

Though it still bugged Laredo that Mary wouldn't tell him her supposed big dark secret, the next morning he didn't have time to dwell on it.

To clear his head, he took his promised ride with Charger, watching the sun rise in a bragging palette of purples and oranges that never failed to stir him.

After a quick check on the chickens and goats—he topped off their water and feed, brought in the eggs, then showered—it was time to find the clothes with "military spirit" that Kyle had requested. He said Laredo should try appealing to eighteen-year-olds intent on giving their lives meaning and adventure.

What did that even mean?

When he'd been eighteen, his only quest had been for beer and babes—not the most admirable of goals.

He chose khaki cargo shorts and a blue T-shirt with NAVY printed on the chest in yellow block letters.

Creaking of the back bedroom door alerted him that he wasn't alone.

He turned, only to gulp at the sight of Mary dressed

in a gauzy nightgown, backlit by golden sun. This was the first he'd noticed her painfully thin frame. Might have been shadows, but were there fading bruises on her upper arms?

"Good morning," she said with her hand to her chest as if he'd given her a scare. "Thought I was the only one up."

"I got an early start. Morning chores are done."

"Good." She nodded.

"It's a long drive into town. We should probably get going."

"About that..." She inched toward the bathroom. "It's probably best if Lark and I stay here. We'd only be in the way."

"Are you sure? You might actually surprise yourself by having fun." He added a hopeful smile.

Was she afraid of a run-in with Kyle?

He almost told her he'd protect her from the sheriff. But was he ready to harbor a fugitive having known her a couple days? No. Carrie taught him women were capable of savage cruelty. Mary might look fragile, but she didn't even try keeping it a secret that she was in hiding. Because of that, he needed to keep her close. Not because he'd looked forward to spending the day with her. Or because she made the thought of reentering his old life infinitely more bearable. Or because he felt almost whole with her by his side. But because she might be dangerous. He needed to ensure she wouldn't bolt. "I want you to come."

"You're sweet. But I figure I'll be better off here. I'll do more deep-cleaning."

"The house has been dirty this long. I figure it can wait a while longer."

"I'm sure it can, but—"

The baby whimpered.

"She still in her crib?" Laredo asked. He'd carried it in last night.

"Yes."

He headed that direction. "You go ahead and use the facilities. I'll take care of your cranky cowgirl."

As if planning a protest, Mary opened her mouth, but then closed it before ducking into the bathroom and closing the door behind her.

Progress? Did this mean she trusted him enough to care for her baby? Or was she desperate enough to escape him that she'd abandon thousands of years of maternal instinct?

Regardless, he scooped the fussy baby from her crib. "Good morning, gorgeous."

Even teary-eyed and huffing, Lark was a brown-eyed beauty like her mom. When Carrie told him she was pregnant, when he wasn't spending time with her, he hung out with his SEAL brothers who had babies and kids. He'd learned to change diapers and feed and bust up squabbles over toys and naptime. Most of all he'd learned just how much he looked forward to becoming a father.

"Where's your dad?" he asked the pint-size angel while setting her on the dresser-turned-changing table. "Wish you could tell me."

After blowing an epic raspberry, she grinned.

"Look at you—showing off your skills. Back in my Navy days, I would have liked to give my CO that same gesture…"

He made quick work of changing her diaper, then snapping her back into her onesie.

Her grin morphed back to tears.

"Aw..." He lifted her into his arms where she nestled her cheek against his shoulder. "Bet you're hungry, huh?"

The bathroom door creaked open.

"There's Mommy..." He turned to face Mary. "I got her diaper changed, but you'll need to take over from here."

"Thanks." She took her daughter from him.

During the exchange, he tried not noticing how good she smelled. Soapy with a floral hint of some feminine lotion. She'd fastened her hair into a high messy bun that somehow managed to look classy and casual.

"She likes you," she said. Her smile was faint, almost wistful.

"I like her." He really did. "Know what would be fun?"

"What?" she asked with a suspicious raising of her eyebrows.

"Feeding her carnival food."

"She's breastfeeding."

"Granted, but hear me out. You know how good funnel cake tastes to us, right?"

"Yes..."

"I'm talking about putting a dusting of powdered sugar on her tongue. Can you imagine the size of her grin?"

Mary tried hiding her smile against the baby's downy curls, but failed.

"Admit it. You think it's a good idea, too. Don't you?"

"Yes, but only because I've secretly been wanting her to try ice cream with fudge sauce—just a little, but enough to tell if she likes it."

"See? This is what I'm talking about. Tag along and keep me company. As an added bonus, we can corrupt your innocent baby."

"You're as incorrigible as a fourth-grader."

"Is that a bad thing? I thought it's good to be in touch with your inner child."

She laughed—a real, honest-to-goodness belly laugh that filled him with pride. "Okay," she said. "Lark and I will go, but under one condition."

"Name it."

"We add corn dogs and Frito chili pie to our list—for us. Not the baby."

"Deal." He held out his hand for her to shake. When their palms touched, the jolt of awareness was as unexpected as it was pleasant. What was it about her that made him want to know more—*everything*—about her? Her favorite foods and songs and books.

She dropped her gaze.

Damn. Had she changed her mind about going?

"What's wrong?"

"Nothing. Just that once my car is fixed, I'll be on my way and that'll be that. You'll forget you even met me."

A sharp pang in his gut told him forgetting her might not be so easy.

*What if I don't want to forget?*

Honestly? If he were taking a deep-down gut check, he wanted her to go to the festival because he couldn't stand being without her and the baby—even for a few hours. He'd been alone for so long that now that he wasn't, the thought of going back scared him. But he couldn't say any of that.

It was hard enough admitting to himself.

This weakness terrified him.

Nighttime terrified him.

Most of all, no longer being the hard-ass, always-in-control SEAL he'd once been terrified him.

Two hours later, Robin found herself seated at a long table placed beneath the welcome shade of an even longer tent, sipping lemonade with Sarah Ziegler, who ran the motel she'd stayed at, and her friend Sally, who was Jimmy the tire guy's fiancée. As foreign as it felt to have left Lark with Laredo, it felt good to have a moment to herself. As much as she loved her baby girl, she'd missed lunching with friends—not that she'd had many after marrying Chuck.

A country trio played on a bandstand.

Four elderly couples decked out in square-dance attire showed off their moves on a portable dance floor.

Balloons and streamers hung from the tent ceiling.

Alternating pots of petunias and marigolds lined each of the three long tables.

The delicious scents of barbecue brisket, roasting ears and funnel cake made her stomach growl.

"Mary, you're welcome to come to our Halloween wedding," Sally said after showing them both photos of her bridal gown. "It's going to be epic. Jimmy and I invited practically the whole town."

"Thanks," Robin said, "but hopefully your guy has me back on the road by then."

"Have you thought of staying around? Back at the recruitment booth, I saw the way Laredo looked at you and your adorable baby."

"It was sweet of him to watch her, giving me this little break. But really, he and I are just friends." *You weren't feeling that way last night when you saw him holding*

*Lark*. "I think his saving my daughter from that carjacker made for an instant connection. He's a good guy."

"The best guy." Sarah sighed, punctuating it with a wistful smile. "Since he first moved here, I wished he'd look my way, but no such luck."

"Have you two been alone?" Robin asked. "Want me to set something up?"

"That's a great idea." Sally leaned forward. "What if I asked him to be your date for the wedding?"

Sarah wrinkled her nose. "That would just be sad. I hate thinking of myself as being that needy."

"How is that needy?" Sally sipped her lemonade. "I see it as doing Laredo a favor by helping him find the beauty that's been right here in front of him all along."

"Makes sense," Robin said. What didn't make sense was how she already regretted this decision to fix Laredo up with another woman. Not that she wanted him—or could even have him. But a selfish part of her didn't want anyone else having him, either.

"I'm going to ask." Sally took out her phone.

"Don't!" Sarah grabbed her friend's wrist. "I changed my mind."

Robin fought not to noticeably exhale with relief.

"Why?" Sally put down her phone.

"Mary—" Sarah turned to her "—don't take this the wrong way, but I've seen the way Laredo looks at you, and if you're his type, then I'm obviously not."

"I promise," Robin confirmed, "nothing has—or will—happen between us. We're friends. Nothing more."

"I get what you're saying, but please understand what I'm getting at. Laredo and I see each other at least once a month around town. If the man wanted to ask me out, he could have on a half-dozen different occasions. I'm guessing tall redheads with freckles aren't his thing."

"His loss." Robin tugged on the long, strawberry blonde braid hanging over Sarah's left shoulder. "I think you're adorable. And crazy sweet."

"I second that vote." Sally patted her friend's hand. "Don't you worry. Jimmy has oodles of single cousins coming for the wedding. I'll bet you take a shining to one of them and by this time next year, we'll all be getting ready for your wedding—well, all of us except for you, Mary. But you could pop back west for a visit."

"Yes, I could," Robin said to be friendly. The truth soured her stomach. Once she left Dandelion Gulch, it would be for good. She would never see these nice women or Laredo again. She barely knew any of them, so why did a knot lurk at the back of her throat?

# *Chapter 7*

"After graduation, why would I join the Navy instead of going on a rodeo circuit?" The gangly kid with too much hair and a mouth too big for his teeth fisted his hands on his hips and set his jaw like he was a tough guy. Or defensive—which was probably closer to the truth. Already considering serving his country, but not quite brave enough to take the plunge.

"Valid question." Laredo shifted the napping baby to his other shoulder. Lord, she felt good—like a grown-up security blanket. "Honestly? If you've got good enough rodeo skills to go professional, I'd choose that route. But if you do a gut check and realize rodeo will never be more than a weekend hobby, you'd probably be better served working toward a real career."

"How come you quit?"

"Excuse me?" Laredo straightened on his folding chair.

"My friend said you were a Navy SEAL but quit."

It was on the tip of Laredo's tongue to feed the kid his standard line about how he'd been honorably discharged. The truth—but not quite the whole truth.

Laredo forced a deep breath. "You're right. I did quit. But not before doing a whole lot of good for my country. What I don't tell many people is that there's a lot more to it. I got hurt. That injury will last me a lifetime. What will also last a good long while? My work ethic. The way I learned to never give up. My love for my SEAL brothers. Truly becoming a man. Nothing about joining will be easy for you, but that's the beauty of it—the harder you work for a goal, the more it means. Do I sometimes have mixed feelings about my time served? Hell, yeah. But I never regret it."

The kid pressed his lips tight and nodded. "That sounds good."

"Right on. Fill out this information card and a recruiter will set up a time to chat."

"Give me one, too," another kid said. His black cowboy hat looked two sizes too big but given time he'd grow into it. Took years for Laredo to fit into his.

By the time his shift ended, he felt surprisingly good about the day.

He took Lark's diaper bag from the back of the booth and hefted it over his shoulder.

"Typical woman," he teased the baby girl. "Always making your man lug around three times as much stuff as you'll ever actually need."

She blew him an adorable raspberry.

"I see how it is. You're flirting me into carrying even more, aren't you?" When he tickled her tummy, she giggled.

"How was it?" Kyle asked. He'd stopped by to refill brochure holders and make sure the guy working the afternoon shift showed up. He had and already occupied Laredo's former seat.

"You know, not half bad. Don't tell anyone, but I actually enjoyed myself."

"I figured you would. Doesn't hurt that you had this little charmer to keep you company. Where's her mom?"

*Avoiding you.* "Mary's around here somewhere. I figured she might enjoy a little time to herself."

"You're a good man." His friend slapped his back. "You'd better stop being such a charmer or this gal's going to declare you caught."

"It's not like that." Laredo adjusted the baby's pink sun hat. Mary dressed her in a frilly pink plaid sunsuit with matching tiny sandals. "We're friends. Nothing more."

"Do you want to be?" Kyle had a special skill for asking painfully awkward direct questions. A good thing for criminal types, but why did he also do it with friends?

"No. And I appreciate you saving your interrogation skills for your office."

"Touchy…" He grinned. "Yep, you want to be more, but feel like you shouldn't. Am I right?"

"On that note…" Laredo exited the booth's canvas shelter with a backhanded wave.

"Hey," Kyle shouted. "Don't leave mad. It's not my fault you wear your heart on your sleeve."

"Keep walking," Laredo mumbled to himself under his breath. What would Kyle know about his heart? Or anyone's for that matter? Had he conveniently forgotten that he was also single?

Laredo passed booth after booth, fighting to not just

regain control, but figure out why he'd lost it. His flash of anger made no sense. Mary was his friend. End of story.

Then he looked up to find her strolling toward him through the crowd. She'd worn her dark hair down and it played hide-and-seek with her brown eyes. Her floral maxi dress clung to her few curves in all the right ways and her smile—her smile revved his pulse and stole his next breath. He'd always thought her to be pretty, but *damn*.

"Sorry I'm late." She slung her small purse over her neck to wear it on her hip, then held out her arms to Lark, who already bucked and grinned to see her mama. "I've been sharing lemonades with Sarah and Sally. We got started on wedding talk and I lost track of time."

"No worries." He fought the urge to hug her, pull her close to brush his lips to the top of her head, and breathe in the clean, floral scent of her hair. He passed her the baby. "We've been taking in the sights. Hungry?"

"Very. I've been teased for hours by the scents drifting from food row."

"What should we try first?"

"Barbecue—and one of those roasting ears. And funnel cake for dessert."

"You got it."

They ate beneath the shade of the big striped tent, enjoying their meal while watching couples square dance to old-school country songs. With the baby fed from bottled breastmilk Mary must have pumped that morning when he'd been tending the animals, Laredo cradled Lark in the crook of his right arm. If pressed, he wasn't sure of the last time he'd felt more at peace.

Mary consulted the day's activity schedule. "If we

hurry, we can just make the last chicken race—assuming you know how to find Larkspur Park?"

"I do, and it's only about a five-minute walk."

"Good. Because as full as I am, if it were any farther, you'd have to roll me."

"Likewise." He winked before shifting Lark to his shoulders, securing her foot with one hand while gathering their plates with his other.

"Let me get that." Mary nudged him aside.

"I can do it."

"Forgive me for doubting your superhero powers, but with my baby six feet off the ground, I'm happy to handle the basics. You focus on safety."

"Yes, ma'am."

They exchanged grins.

What would it be like for days like this to be his new normal? This wasn't his usual scene, but with Mary and Lark, it felt good. Almost normal save for the fact that she would soon be gone.

"You okay?" Mary asked after taking their trash to the bin.

"Sure. Why?"

"All of the sudden you look…ferocious."

"I'm good. Great." He forced a smile, then did what felt natural by holding out his hand.

At first, she seemed taken aback by his gesture. Looking down and then away, but then lightly pressing her palm to his. The sensation was all at once electrifying yet calming. Thrilling yet soothing. He didn't know how, but without even trying, she and Lark calmed the beast roaring in his head. The one still angry about Carrie and losing his night vision and forever being alone.

With her, for now, he was once again part of something bigger than himself and it didn't just feel good, but sublime.

But that was every bit as much of an illusion as her smile.

What he needed to remember was that she had secrets. Secrets possibly more explosive than any bomb he'd detonated while on active duty.

Holding Laredo's hand tightened Robin's throat. Sharing this sun-drenched afternoon, watching him with Lark in his arms produced a keen longing that was nearly too much to bear.

This was the way her life was supposed to have turned out.

Instead, she'd been beaten and humiliated and forced to do something she'd never dreamed possible. Because of that, her life had now spun in an entirely new direction. All she had was today and tomorrow before her car would be repaired and she would resume the forward momentum necessary to carry Lark to safety.

Freedom.

But until then…

She swallowed hard, brushing tears from her eyes before Laredo saw. Until then, she would allow this dream to play out in glorious Technicolor.

On their way to the races, they passed a small carnival midway with whirling rides blasting rock music and screaming teens. There were barkers calling out for folks to try their games. Teasing whiffs of cotton candy and popcorn made her hungry all over again.

Often Laredo ran into friends.

Each time, he'd introduce her and Lark, explaining that she was the woman who'd been carjacked. News must have spread fast as everyone greeted her effusively, apologizing before assuring her nothing like that had ever happened in their small town.

Through it all, Robin held tight to Laredo's hand. She wanted to believe herself strong, but when she thought she'd caught sight of Kyle, her pounding heart told her she wasn't at all strong, but a coward who had no business dragging Laredo into her mess.

When they reached the grassy park where the races were being held, Laredo led her to the top row on a set of small bleachers facing the historic blond brick courthouse, shaded by majestic cottonwoods.

A ten-foot-wide course had been established using chicken wire draped in red, white and blue bunting. At one end of the twenty-yard course stood six antsy owners and their hens.

"How does this work?" she asked Laredo.

"It doesn't. *Bedlam* is the best way to describe it. The owners will get out in front of their hens, jogging backward to try coaxing them toward the finish. I've seen some folks have luck using worms. Sometimes the chickens just wander and the race takes an hour or more. Other times, a hen gets spooked and charges straight for the finish line."

"Ever think of entering one of your hens?"

He laughed. "My crew are too fat and lazy."

"Aw, that's not nice."

"But true." He smiled again before lowering Lark to his lap. "They're about to start. Care to place a friendly wager?"

"I would, but—" her smile faded "—I don't have cash to spare."

"Let's make it more interesting by raising the stakes.

I'm talking way higher than mere money. If you win, I'll cook dinner and do dishes. I win, you get the honors."

"Hmm..." Head cocked, she considered her odds. "Since you're the only one of us who's ever even heard of a chicken race, how is that fair? How do I pick a winner?"

"I'll never tell." Stealing her breath with a slow and easy grin, he teased, "Of course, if you're too chicken to place a simple bet, then we can just watch."

"Oh—them's fighting words."

"Ladies first—choose who you think will dominate."

Robin took a moment to ponder her choices. "I'm going for the teen with pigtails and overalls. She looks young enough to be especially spry. Plus, see the way she holds her hen? They seem connected on a deeper level than some of her competition."

"Fair enough," he said. "I respect your opinion, but I'm thinking the clear choice is the grandfatherly sort who's been whispering to his hen while feeding her dandelions. Ned says they're like chicken tranquilizers. Nice and calming."

"Yeah, but isn't the point for the hens to be speedy?"

Dawning was slow to come, but when it did, he slapped his knee and cursed under his breath. "You make a valid point."

Grinning, she asked, "Care to change your bet?"

"Absolutely. I'm going with the guy in the sleeveless Metallica T-shirt with all the tattoos and a mullet."

"Final answer? They're about to start..."

He nodded. "I'm sure he's the winner." Glancing at the baby, he added, "Lark agrees."

"I'll bet she does." As all six hens and their handlers approached the starting line, Robin couldn't quit smiling. When was the last time she'd had this much fun? Far too long ago.

Sadly, once she left, she might not feel this carefree for many more years to come. Fighting to put that reality aside in favor of savoring the here and now, she leaned forward, resting her elbows on her knees.

A referee dressed in black and white stepped up to a microphone. "Let's keep this a clean, family-fun race. No elbowing fellow handlers or shouting obscenities. If you wouldn't do it in church, don't do it here. Everyone understand?"

Laredo leaned close. "He refs the high school football and basketball games during the week, then preaches on Sunday. In his spare time, he also handles weddings and funerals."

"Impressive," Robin said with a smile.

"On your marks… Get set… *Go!*"

Bluegrass played over a loudspeaker while all six chickens wandered the course—none in too big of a hurry to complete the race.

The crowd went wild, shouting for their favorites as most hens seemed content to forage for worms and bugs rather than listen to their handlers.

"Come on, Pigtail Girl!" Like everyone around her, Robin stood.

Laredo followed her lead. "Run, Metallica Man! *Run!*"

After at least ten minutes of coaxing and cajoling, the grandfather reached into one of his baggy overalls pockets and pulled out a couple of marigold blossoms.

His hen caught sight of them and perked right up.

"Is that fair?" Robin asked.

"Unfortunately, yes."

The older gentleman backward shuffled all the way to the finish line, where he gave his hen her prize.

"We have a winner!" The announcer gifted the winning hen with a tiny sash that read: *WING-DING CHAMPION!*

"We both lost," Laredo said.

"What do we do for dinner now?" Robin asked.

"Share the workload?"

"Deal."

The crowd pressed them together, with Lark giggling and cooing between them.

Robin looked up to find her lips mere inches from his. In the moment, nothing seemed more natural, more desirable, than standing on her tiptoes to close that gap. He tilted his head, as if fully planning to meet her halfway.

Heart pounding, mouth dry, Robin struggled for her next erratic breath. In the heart of this boisterous crowd, it felt as if she and Laredo were the only two souls left on earth. Much to her secret shame, she liked it. The last time she'd been with Chuck was long before Lark had been born. Right after he'd last forced himself on her, she'd left him and filed a restraining order.

Her every instinct told her that if she and Laredo did share a kiss, nothing would ever feel more right. All she had to do was rise up. Lean in. Take a deep breath and let herself fall…

She'd grown perilously close to doing all of that when a voice called from the crowd. "Hey, Laredo! Thought you two were just friends?"

Laredo was once again mumbling curses.

Kyle stood on the grass beside the bleachers. No matter how desperately she wanted to run, Robin knew there was no escaping him.

At some point between the time she'd almost kissed Laredo and now, the crowd had thinned.

Kyle beamed up at them as if he were a woman at a crowded beauty shop, intent on wagging what he saw as a gossipy bone. "Don't stop on my account."

Laredo glared.

"Need help?" Kyle held out his hand to help her down.

Not wanting to raise his suspicions by being rude, she took his hand, dropping it the instant she stood on firm ground.

Tipping his uniform hat back, Kyle said, "I'm on my way to pick up a couple guys who had too many beers, but since I saw you, I wanted to thank you again for helping with the recruitment booth. You had fifteen young men fill out forms of intent and three young women. That's a record."

Laredo whistled. "Nice."

"You'd better watch out. With numbers like that, the Navy might want you back."

He chuckled. "They can want all they want, but I'm happy on my homestead."

"Understood. You two enjoy the rest of your afternoon."

"Will do," Laredo said with a wave.

"That's great," Robin said. "What did you tell those teens that garnered so much interest?"

"The truth." Lips pressed into a thin line, he said, "I didn't glamorize what's a seriously dangerous job, but told them despite the good and bad, I had no regrets. Who knows? Maybe straight talk piqued their curiosity enough to give it a try."

"Maybe."

"How are you?" He nudged her shoulder with his. "I know you'd planned to avoid Kyle."

"True. But like most worries, this turned out to be no big deal."

"Are you saying you don't really have cause to fear a confrontation with him?"

*I wish.* "Let's just say that unless he's specifically looking, he'd have no reason to believe I'm anything other than a single mom on her way for a nice visit with her grandparents."

Walking side by side, they headed back toward the carnival midway. Lark had fallen asleep, resting her flushed cheek on Laredo's shoulder.

Robin's chest swelled from the sweet sight.

"But if he did take a closer look at you—even going so far as to do a computer search using your real name—you feel fairly certain he wouldn't like what he finds?"

# *Chapter 8*

*Shut up!* Laredo told himself, so why the hell wouldn't his lips quit yapping? The moment he'd asked the question, Mary's suddenly pale expression told him he'd hit a painful nerve. "Never mind," he said. "Forget the whole issue."

She froze.

"Mary, really. It's okay. Whatever you did, whoever you were, I don't want to know. First thing Monday morning, I'll run you over to Jimmy's, he'll fix your tires and you'll be on your way. The two of us will most likely never see each other again."

Nodding, she swallowed hard.

Her big brown eyes welled with tears.

"What's wrong?"

"I'm going to miss you."

Likewise. "Maybe I could come see you in Arkansas. I've never been. Ned and Augusta could watch the goats and chickens."

She shook her head. "That would never work."

"Why not?"

"It just wouldn't."

"Try me."

"It's complicated. Beyond messy."

"While in the Navy, messy was my specialty."

"I don't doubt you'd come out the hero in any given situation, but there's nothing the least bit heroic about what I've done." Head bowed, more tears flowed.

They'd made it to the midway. He dodged ten feet to the left to take a few napkins from a holder alongside a hot dog stand.

"Hey!" the clerk called through the food truck's open side window. "Those are for customers only!"

Laredo kept right on walking.

"Here." After handing Mary the wad of paper, he backed her onto a bench, shielding her from passersby. Shadows were lengthening, and the crowd had transitioned from families to couples attending that night's concert. Three bands would be playing and the carnival rides kept spinning till midnight. "You do know there's nothing I can do to help if you don't tell me what's wrong?"

She nodded.

Three youngish teen guys raced past.

Five squealing girls chased after them.

The sudden noise that was even louder than the racket drifting from the midway woke Lark with a start.

Laredo tried jiggling and rocking her back to sleep, but she wasn't having it.

"Let me have her." Mary sniffled and dried her eyes.

"Sorry for my meltdown. Yesterday and today have been such a stark contrast to what my life has been that it reminded me what I've been through isn't normal. This—being with you at a cheesy festival, making silly bets on whether or not a chicken will run—is the sort of idyllic life I've been searching for. This day is the kind of thing I wanted Lark growing up remembering." She teared up again but blotted her eyes. "I can only pray she never remembers a single thing about her father."

"What did he do?" Still jiggling the baby, Laredo sat beside her. "It's just me and you here." And it was. There might have been a crowd of a couple thousand, but there was anonymity to be found amongst the sea of people.

"M-my name isn't Mary."

He nodded. "Not a surprise."

"I-it's Robin."

"Nice meeting you, Robin. When you're ready, tell me what Lark's father did that scared you bad enough to make you take on an assumed identity."

"I can't."

"Can't or won't?" He didn't mean to snip at her. If fact, if he was a gentleman, he'd have offered to make a solo hike to the truck, picking up her and the baby for the long trek home. But if he left them, given her current skittish behavior, there was no guarantee they'd be here when he came back. "Sorry. Forget I asked. Let's get to the truck and head home. It will be dark soon. I don't like driving at night."

"I'm sorry."

"Stop apologizing. You didn't do anything wrong." *That I know of.* The truth was murkier. He didn't have a clue what she'd really done. The longer she kept her big secret, the more he wondered just how serious her actions may have been. He had to find out. That was the only way to save her. "Come on. Let's go."

He held out his hand.

She accepted.

For the moment, Lark's wide-eyed fascination with the bright midway lights took precedence over her cries. Thank God. Laredo couldn't handle two crying females at once.

It took thirty minutes to reach the truck.

Another hour to escape the congested field-turned-parking lot.

By the time he steered the truck onto the main highway leading out of the chaotic town, the sky was streaked with orange, purple and red. Any ordinary man would look at such a spectacular sun setting over distant mountains with a smile.

The majestic sight made Laredo scowl.

He had about fifteen minutes until his peripheral vision grew nonexistent and his front sightlines narrowed to maybe a ten-foot swath. Basically, he could see the width of a chicken race lane. Just what a man wanted when charged with his family's safety.

Only Lark and Robin weren't his.

Would never be his.

Why couldn't he get that fact through his thick skull?

With both ladies dozing, Laredo punched the gas on the paved road, trying to save precious daylight for the dirt road to come. For the most part, the trip was a straight shot. But the higher in elevation they got, the more twists, turns and drop-offs there were.

Twenty minutes later, darkness had fallen.

He switched on the high beams, but they were no match for his condition.

Sweat popped out on his forehead.

His heart hammered.

His vision had tunneled to the point that he'd slowed the truck to a fifteen-miles-per-hour crawl. At this rate, he wouldn't reach the homestead till Christmas. It had been irresponsible of him to let this happen. He should have told Mary—correction, Robin—that the last races were too late. That they needed to be on the road before then. But he'd been too damned busy contemplating kissing her to consider the ramifications of what delaying their exit truly meant.

The harder he stared at the road, the worse his vision grew until his line of sight narrowed to a measly five feet. He could no longer see either side of the road—just barely enough to keep going.

One at a time, he removed his trembling hands from the wheel to wipe his sweating palms on the thighs of his jeans. Time and distance stretched into an endless tunnel through which he couldn't find his bearings. Were they fifteen minutes from home or fifteen hours?

He *hated* this.

Being weak.

Incapable of providing adequate care for the two gals who had in such a brief time grown to be important fixtures in his life.

"Laredo?" Robin's voice drifted to him as if it passed through a dense fog. Was he losing his hearing, too? "Are you okay?"

He couldn't answer. If he took his attention from the road, there was no telling what could happen. There could be a five-hundred-foot cliff mere inches from either tire. One false move and he'd kill them all.

His heart beat faster and harder until he realized

the truck was no longer moving at all. Just his chest—struggling to find his next breath.

"What's wrong?" asked a feminine voice through the ether. "How can I help?"

"I—I can't see." His voice was hoarse. His tone defeated. *"I can't see."*

"It's okay," she said. "It's not, but you know what I mean. Let's trade places. I have good night vision. My best guess is we're still about thirty minutes from your place. The landscape is nice and flat here with plenty of room for us to get out and switch." She leaned forward, wrapping her hand around his that gripped the wheel so tight he wasn't sure he could ever let go. "But even if it weren't, there's not a lot of traffic, right?"

*"I c-can't s-see..."* He didn't want to break down. He refused to break down. She needed a real man—not some busted-ass imposter of the man he used to be. Tears stung his eyes but he refused to let them spill.

"Since your foot's already on the brake, I'm putting the truck in Park. Okay?"

He nodded.

He flinched when her arm crossed his stomach.

"It's okay," she said. "I'm opening your door. The truck is safely in Park. All you need to do is inch out. I'm right here. Hold my hand."

When he clasped her hand to his, he laced their fingers, holding her like she was his only lifeline, because at this moment, she was.

"You've got this. A little farther..."

He slid off the familiar bench seat until the soles of his cowboy boots hit the ground.

Still holding his hand, he felt the jolt as she landed beside him.

When she wrapped her arms around his waist, holding him close, unwanted release shattered his self-control. Tears of frustration and rage and sorrow flowed. This wasn't how his life was supposed to have turned out. Compared to other guys he knew, he had it lucky. He had most of his vision and all his limbs. Why couldn't he get his shit together? Why had he chosen now to throw himself a pity party?

"It's okay," she said. "Everything's going to be okay."

"I'm sorry. I hate letting you down."

"Letting me down?" Voice raspy, she said, "You're my hero. You not only saved my daughter from a carjacker, but you're providing us food, shelter and fun. You're amazing."

"Stop."

"No, you stop. So you've got an issue with your night vision. Big deal."

"It is—it's a freaking huge deal."

"Know what? Compared to the fact that I killed my husband, it's nothing."

He froze.

She released him, then took a step back. Through his narrowed line of sight, in the headlights' glow, he saw her raise trembling hands to cover her mouth.

"There it is," she said. "My big secret."

"What do you mean, you killed him? Like shot him or what?"

She shook her head. "Nothing like that. But his parents fully blame me. I had a restraining order against him, but that night he was angry about a band canceling at the last minute for a big show. He showed up at my apartment drunk, demanding to see Lark. When I refused him, he kicked in the door. He never hit my face—never wanted proof of what he'd done—but he grabbed me by my upper arms, shoving me to the floor. He kicked me over and over. I knew not to scream or cry or even whimper until his rage was spent. Once it was, and he'd locked himself in the bathroom, I grabbed Lark and my purse and bolted for my car. Because of my fear, I kept emergency supplies and cash in the trunk. I was backing out of the driveway when he darted out after us. Not thinking of anything other than keeping me and my baby safe, I just drove. When I heard another car's horn and screeching brakes..."

"So he was hit?"

"Yeah. Instantly killed."

"Good riddance."

"That night, after the police questioning and dealing with his parents, I couldn't bear going back to my apartment—knowing it was trashed. That night, Lark and I stayed in a hotel, but I got zero sleep. Chuck's father's accusations kept circling in my head. He accused me of making his son crazy. Said if I'd been a better wife, he'd still be alive. He even called me an unfit mother—threatened to sue for full custody of Lark. I was so scared that when he made the custody threat again at the funeral I had no choice but to run. I can't live without my baby..."

She broke down.

"Come here..." Now, Laredo was the one pulling her into his arms. His pulse had calmed and knowing her secret made him all the more determined to save her. He hadn't imagined those fading bruises he'd seen that morning. But with her ex in the ground and her father-in-law's threats most likely empty, her days of worry and fear were behind her. "Everything's going to be okay."

She nodded against his chest.

"Get us home, then just to give you added peace of mind, I'll do an online search for California custody laws concerning grandparents. After that, we'll plan our next move."

"W-wouldn't that be *my* next move?"

"Not anymore. If you want, I'll be with you every step of the way." Earlier, his heart raced because of his poor vision, but now, it thundered for an entirely different reason—he feared her telling him she'd rather go it alone.

"Thank you," Robin said. "I'd like that." It was odd thinking of herself as her true identity as opposed to Mary—the woman for whom she'd purchased a driver's license and practiced using her name. Honestly? The whole plan to involve her grandparents in hiding her from Chuck's parents had been ill-conceived from the start. They'd cautioned her against running off with her former husband, but she'd believed herself madly in love. She'd been incapable of seeing anything other than his larger-than-life persona. He considered some of the biggest names in country and rock to be close friends. What would he see in a small-town bumpkin like her?

What had he seen? A malleable, naive young woman over whom he believed he'd exerted ultimate control. Only she'd taken it back—for a short while. Although if his parents did somehow take her baby, tragically, even from his grave he'd have ultimately won.

"Well..." She forced a deep, shuddering breath. "Should we get going? We're probably on borrowed time until Lark realizes it's an hour past her dinnertime and wakes with a vengeance."

"Sure." He brushed past her to climb into the truck,

easing to the bench seat's center. "You'll need to adjust the seat. The control switch is on the side."

"Good to know." Sitting behind the wheel of Laredo's truck felt beyond odd, and she did use the magic button to bring her right foot closer to the gas and brake pedals.

He sat ramrod straight with his arms crossed.

"How are you doing?" she asked after putting the truck in gear and easing up to speed.

"Let's just say it's been quite a night—for us both."

"You are beyond kind—helping me."

"Any decent human would."

"Sadly, even though my apartment complex houses hundreds of people, not a single one stepped in to help." Not entirely true. How many times had Mrs. Jerome called police, but Robin refused to press charges? But how could she when her ex threatened to kill her and Lark if she ever exposed his monstrous actions. "You're a good man, Laredo. The best."

He snorted. "Unless you need help at night."

"I'm going to pretend you didn't say that."

"Pretend all you want, but if your ex arose from the dead and showed up here itching for a fight, I'd have to tell him to stand beneath the floodlights just to see his ugly face clear enough to punch it."

Robin thanked God their situation would never escalate to that degree. But since she was glad Chuck died, did that make her the true monster?

# *Chapter 9*

While Robin nursed Lark on the living room sofa, Laredo had volunteered to cook a simple supper of a ham steak he'd defrosted in the microwave along with boxed mac and cheese and canned green beans. They'd probably ingest more vitamins and minerals eating a handful of dirt, but at least they wouldn't go to bed with growling stomachs.

By the time he'd finished, Robin had fed the baby, given her a quick bath, then dressed her in a fresh diaper and onesie before tucking her into the portable crib.

Laredo still felt awkward as hell about the way things had gone down in the truck. More than anything, he hated feeling vulnerable—correction, he hated showing anyone else that he was feeling vulnerable. Typically he was better able to hide his insecurities.

"Thank you for cooking." She entered the living room, looking pretty but weary in gray sweatpants and an off-the-shoulder T-shirt that showed a glimpse of yellowish bruising until she yanked it up.

"Sure. No problem. Have a seat and I'll fix you a plate."

"Thanks." She pulled out a chair and all but collapsed.

"Did the peanut fall right off to sleep?"

"You know it. She had a busy day."

"We all did." He set two heaping plates on the table, then doubled back for forks, knives and napkins. "Wish we had more of your stew. You'd win in a cook-off."

"We're not having a contest." She still hadn't picked up her fork. "Can we please stop dancing around the elephant sharing the seat beside me."

"Remember? I can't see." He forked a huge bite and chewed.

"That's not funny. I could be on the verge of an ugly custody battle."

"You don't know that." He pushed his chair back. "Want a beer?"

"Yes, but unfortunately I can't drink while nursing."

"That sucks, but I applaud your dedication."

He rejoined her before unscrewing the top of the long-neck brew, then taking a deep swig. "Okay, the way I see it, we finish our meals, then I'll open my laptop and we'll check out those California laws. If we think your ex's folks may have a legitimate claim, we'll weigh your options. If not, we'll weigh those options. Either way, there's nothing we can do tonight, so we might as well enjoy our supper—as lackluster as it is."

"If only all of this was that simple."

"It is. From what you told me, I truly believe the worst is behind you."

She nodded, but still didn't eat.

He speared a few orange noodles with his fork, then reached across the table. Holding the food to her lips, he said, *"Please..."*

She took the bite and chewed.

After swallowing, she asked, "How much butter did you put in that? It tastes suspiciously naughty."

"I figured you could use a little meat on your bones."

"True. And thanks—not just for this delicious comfort food, but everything." Her sad laugh shattered him. "First thing Monday morning, Lark and I will be gone."

He took a moment for this to sink in.

All of it.

His mishmash of feelings for her and her daughter. The fact that she'd just lost her ex. No way was she ready for a new relationship—not that he was, either. Just sayin'.

"What are you thinking?" While moving her mac and cheese from one part of her plate to another, she didn't meet his gaze.

"Nothing important." *Liar.*

"Sorry to have dragged you into this mess. I never should have told you." She shook her head. "I'm not even sure why I did."

"Does it matter?"

Shrugging, she finally took a bite.

He pushed back his chair and stood. "Hang tight."

"Where are you going?"

"To get my laptop."

More than anything, Lark wanted to forcibly stop Laredo from ruining the sanctity of this place. This night.

Even with Chuck dead, she felt as if her nightmare with him might never end.

He'd been charismatic and charming when they'd first met. Attentive. Always bringing her little gifts meant to show how much he cared. In hindsight, they'd really represented the degree to which he studied her every move.

"Are you ready for this?" Laredo asked upon his return. He plugged in a slim computer, then rejoined her at the table.

"If I said no, would you stop?"

"I could, but would that do any good? If I'm going to help improve your situation, we kind of need to know what the situation is. Agreed?"

Swallowing the knot lurking at the back of her throat, she nodded. As soon as he typed *custody rights + grandparents + California* into his search engine, her stomach churned.

"How long have you been divorced?" he asked while sifting through results.

"A whole month. Chuck fought it, but I fought just as hard." Not that the piece of paper documenting her freedom meant anything. He'd still come and gone as he liked and shared custody of Lark. If anything, the legalization of their split had upped his head game. He'd stalk her, waiting to catch her alone to deliver discreet blows. The few times her neighbor called police, he had ready alibis and alternate explanations of how she'd gotten her bruises. Falling. Running into the table edge. Slamming her arm in the car door. He'd so matter-of-factly explained it all away that she'd begun to fear for her sanity.

While Laredo typed and clicked, Robin's pulse pounded.

She could just have easily searched for the information on her smartphone, but she hadn't wanted to know.

This time free from her worries had been too precious to allow her past to intrude.

"I'm just scanning, but from what I'm seeing, for your in-laws to have a case, they'd have to prove you unfit." He read more. "This is probably the last thing you want to hear, but I think you should go back to California. The fact that you took off without telling them could be a problem."

The thought of returning to her trashed apartment made her shiver. She couldn't do it. Chuck may be dead, but he would still be there—in every piece of broken furniture and every spilled drop of her blood.

"You okay?"

Tearing, she nodded.

"But see?" He went to her, dropping to his knees to clasp her hands. "Since you're a great mom, as soon as you return to California—at least long enough to assure Lark's grandparents that they're welcome to see her—they should legally have no rights beyond basic visitation."

"I should—go back. But..." Squealing tires and that blaring car horn reverberated through her head. Then she saw Chuck. Lifeless. Circled in blood. "I need more time—just to process everything I've been through. As soon as my car is fixed, I should be on my way to Arkansas. But that feels overwhelming, too." Eyes closed, she sighed. "I'm tired. Exhausted on a soul-deep level. I'm not even sure if it's safe for me to drive that far of a distance."

"So stay—just for a little while. Till you feel better. Totally on your own terms."

On her own terms...

Had there ever been a sweeter phrase in all of the English language?

How easy it would be to stay. How seductive. This place's peace and isolation served as a healing balm. Laredo's strength and support an even better medicine.

"Well?" He squeezed her hands.

After a slow exhale, she nodded.

But then shook her head. "Thank you so much for this offer. But I need time to think." *Breathe.* "For now, let's just pretend Lark and I are staying. I would insist on helping out. What would be our first task?"

"Clearly..." Releasing her hands, he settled back into the seat across from her. "Lark's job description would be in a predominantly supervisory capacity. You and I would both report directly to her."

"Of course." Was it possible for a person's soul to smile? She'd known him such a brief time, but Laredo made her happy.

Deep in her belly a warning chimed.

Her smile faded.

Chuck had once made her happy. They'd married after knowing each other only eight weeks. When it came to men, Robin's instincts couldn't be trusted. Why should her blossoming feelings for Laredo be different?

"What's wrong? As Lark's representative, if you feel the goats and chickens should also report to her, I'll see what can be arranged."

Robin forced a sad smile. Sad, because she wanted—craved—this lighthearted banter. She'd grown beyond weary of her gloomy day-to-day existence. Skittering like a scared mouse, always wondering when Chuck would next pounce. But for Lark's sake, for her own, she had to slow this thing with Laredo—whatever it was.

"Your terms are more than adequate," she said. "I just can't rush into anything. Please understand this has nothing to do with you. I've only just emerged from a nightmare. I need a minute to fully wake."

"I get it." He reached across the table for her hand.

At first, she hesitated, but then she reached for him, too. When their fingers intertwined, the sensation was akin to coming home. An emotional sigh.

"When I realized the extent of my vision issues, I wasn't sure how to react. As a SEAL, most missions are clandestine—carried out under a nice, dark cover. I used to love night. The way it provided a sort of superhero invisibility cloak. Now, I've been stripped of those powers and darkness is my enemy. I had to relearn everything. All I knew was how to be a soldier."

"But look at you. This place is fantastic and given time, it's only going to get better." He stroked her palm with his thumb, striking a spark she feared could lead to an all-consuming fire. A womanly yearning clenched low in her belly. Her breath hitched and pulse quickened. How long had it been since she'd had a satisfying sexual experience? Too long. "You're lucky—having a special place to call your own."

He focused on their still clasped hands. "I used to think so, but truth is, I get lonely. I never planned on living out here on my own. Having you and Lark has been a welcome respite from reality. But if you stayed… Just long enough to build up your energy."

He raised his gaze to meet hers. The intensity. The heat. It was all nearly too much to bear.

She licked her lips. "I'll think about it. Promise."

"No. I'm sorry." He released her hand to close his laptop. "You've just emerged from a crisis. You should be with family. In fact, you and Lark could fly. I'll deal with your car. Yes—family. That's most important."

*What if in some crazy, topsy-turvy way you've become my family?*

"Thank you." When he'd given her an easy out, why did her throat tighten with disappointment. Was he regretting his offer? "It is probably best if I leave. I'll drink plenty of coffee and should be fine to drive. Grandma and Grandpa are expecting me."

"Of course." He pushed back his chair. Grabbed both of their plates.

"Let me do that." She also rose. "You cooked. It's only fair I clean."

"Not necessary."

"Oddball confession time—washing dishes relaxes me. I love the warm, soapy water."

He laughed. "For real?"

"Yep. Growing up, the dishwasher was me. Grandma and Grandpa would be in the living room, watching their shows or talking. Sometimes playing cards with friends. I loved hearing them happy and feeling part of our tight-knit family—however small."

"They sound like good people."

"They are. I miss them."

"I'm sure they miss you. When's the last time they've seen you and Lark?"

"They flew out for her birth. After the divorce, they urged me to return to their home, but per my custody agreement with Chuck, I couldn't leave the county."

"Wow."

"Yeah." She ran the water, putting her fingers beneath the flow, waiting till it warmed to put the stopper in the drain and add soap.

"But that's no longer an issue."

"Is it wrong that I'm not sad he died? He has friends

and family. Parents who dearly loved him. Dozens if not hundreds of powerful friends in the entertainment business. None of them knew the monster he was."

"Tell them."

"What would be the point? He's gone. I'm free. wouldn't it be kinder to let them remember him in a happy way?"

"Not to you. Why did they think you divorced?"

"I told them irreconcilable differences. If I'd told the truth, he threatened to…" How long would it take his threats to stop circling her memories? *Cross me, tell a soul about what you perceive to be the truth, and I'll effing slit your throat. There won't be a custody issue, because Lark will no longer have a bitch for a mother. I'll let you have your divorce, but if you think you'll ever leave me, you're sorely mistaken. Wait—even better, I'll slit Lark's tiny throat in front of you…* She shook her head and forced a smile. "Doesn't matter. The nightmare is over and I'm ready to start my shiny new fear-free life."

"I'm so sorry for what he put you through." He carried the pots and pans from the stove. "Bastard should've rotted in a cell."

"Can we please not talk about it?"

"Right. Sorry."

"Quit apologizing for another man's actions. You've been nothing but good to me and my daughter. You'll never know how grateful I am."

"Glad I was here to help." He scooped the mac and cheese leftovers into a plastic container, then snapped on a lid.

"What should we do tomorrow? Since it's our last day, you should put us to work."

"How is Lark with a hammer?"

"Depends. Would you like her to lick it or use it for teething?"

"Yeah, maybe we'll stick with having her supervise."

"Good call."

They shared a laugh. It felt amazing for the mood to have once again lightened.

Setting the last fork in the dish strainer, Robin asked, "What do you have planned for the hammer?"

"I thought we'd start my new goat shed. This heat won't last forever, and once winter comes, those mamas will be awfully cold."

"I'm happy to be your gopher, but I'm not sure how much help I'll actually be."

"Relax. It's not the Taj Mahal. Just a simple goat shed."

For the briefest moment she closed her eyes, gripping the counter's edge. *When it comes to my mixed-up feelings for you, Laredo, nothing's simple.*

More and more she realized leaving him would be very hard.

As soon as the sun gifted him with enough light to see, Laredo, dressed in Wranglers and a white T-shirt, slapped on his cowboy hat, crammed his feet into his favorite black boots, then left the house to saddle Charger.

The tightness in his chest made him want to race the chestnut across the vast open space, galloping out his frustrations, but that wouldn't be fair to his horse. With prairie dog and snake holes, he couldn't take a chance on the beast being hurt.

Instead, he followed his favorite trail winding north of the house until circling a butte through sagebrush, milkweed and sunflowers. This early, the sun kissed the butte's reddish-orange face to such an extent that it glowed.

Charger knew the familiar trail and followed it to the top, where he also knew Laredo would climb off, leaving him free to graze on the sweet clover patch thriving alongside the red rocks where Laredo did his best thinking.

With no wind and a sky so blue he could see clear to forever, when Laredo finally left his horse and took a seat, he'd already begun to feel better.

It had been a long night—entirely caused by trouble of his own making. What had he been thinking, inviting Robin and her baby to stay? As much as he'd enjoyed their company, he barely knew the woman.

Hell, he'd been married to Carrie and couldn't make that work. What made him think he was ready for a live-in relationship with a stranger?

He wasn't.

Which was why he'd been relieved when she turned down his offer. The problem that had kept him up all night was wondering why, then, that relief had turned to dread for her and the baby's eventual leaving.

Lord, he was tired of being alone. Eating alone. Riding alone. Gardening alone. That was the sole reason he was so worked up about this issue, right?

Surely, any woman would do.

Only, if that was true, then how come he hadn't taken up Lulu on her not-so-subtle offers? Or any of the other single ladies in town? As much as he hated to admit it, something about Robin touched him in a long-forgotten place he never thought he'd see again.

She made him want to do better—more. Get the house

spit-shined and polished. Maybe plant a few flowers. Put a fresh coat of paint on the house and front-porch swing where they could while away long summer nights.

But because she was leaving, none of that would happen. And that was okay. It wasn't as if he'd die if she didn't stay. If anything, his energy would be better spent improving things that mattered. Not the house, but the garden and goats and learning to put up his crops for winter.

Yes. That was a solid plan.

A realistic plan.

So why did he still feel like shit?

"We make an epic team," Laredo said to Robin late Sunday morning while standing back to survey the finished foundation. The rectangular form had been easy enough to make, but mixing ten bags of concrete, then smoothing it out, had been a bear in the day's growing heat. "Know what I think we should do before it dries?"

"Take a break?" Robin grinned. She'd worked every bit as hard as he had, and her tousled hair showed it—not that he was complaining. Flushed from the heat, her complexion glowed.

Lark cooed in her carrier that her mama had parked in the cottonwood's shade.

The goats complained in the temporary pen Laredo made from a spare roll of chicken wire.

"Since the concrete has to cure for a while, we're at a forced stopping point."

"Whew." Feigning exhaustion, she wiped her brow.

"Was it really that bad?"

"Yes!" She laughed. "But I'm proud of what we accomplished."

"Me, too. But I want to do one more thing before we head inside."

"Name it."

"Let's make Lark's handprint in the drying cement. That way, when you two find time for a visit, she can see how much she's grown." Sounded reasonable, but he also wanted the reminder for himself. He wanted tangible proof that the infant and her mom hadn't been a mirage.

"Sounds fun. Let's do it."

Laredo made the short trek to pluck the baby from her carrier, then returned her to what would soon be the goat estate's grand entrance. Kneeling, he asked Robin, "You want to do the honors?"

"Go ahead." Her smile made the project even more special. But also bittersweet. This time tomorrow, they would both be gone. Chest suddenly tight, he ignored the pain of them leaving to embrace the here and now. The scent of baby shampoo in Lark's hair. The feel of her slight weight cradled in his arms. The air of wonder stemming from one look at Robin's smile. In this moment, all was right in his world, and if this was all he would ever have, then so be it.

On his knees, he held Lark's tiny hand to the freshly smoothed concrete.

Robin kneeled beside him, leaning close, pressing her shoulder to his. The connection revved his pulse.

It made the sunlight brighter. The air fresher.

"This was a great idea."

"Want to write her name beneath the print?"

Grinning, she nodded.

He leaned back for a twig, handing it to her.

"Thanks." She lingered over the letters, making sure

they looked just right. Finished, she sat back on her heels. Her smile reached her eyes. “Perfect.”

*Just like you…*

He turned to her and she to him. His next breath hung—trapped in his chest like the sparks her proximity created. He wanted to kiss her. Needed to kiss her. Leaning closer, heart pounding, he’d almost touched his lips to hers when the sound of tires crunching on the gravel drive pulled him away. “Damn.”

She cleared her throat before lowering her gaze.

“What the hell?” Still holding the baby, Laredo rose. “What’s he doing here?”

When Kyle stopped his official police SUV in front of the house, dread fisted low in Laredo’s belly. Was this a friendly visit or could it be something more?

# *Chapter 10*

"Give me Lark." Robin thrust out her arms. "I need to run. *Hide.*"

"No, you don't. You've done nothing wrong. Kyle's my friend. He's probably here on a social call. Maybe he's got another recruitment event he wants me to work."

"I—I can't risk it." Just like that, everything changed. One moment she'd been close to kissing her dream man, the next, she'd slipped right back into her nightmare. "Give me my baby. Maybe he hasn't seen me yet."

"You're being irrational. Come on." He took her hand, but she jerked it free.

"You're playing fast and loose with my life."

"Hey!" Kyle waved before starting toward them.

"Great," she mumbled under her breath. Heart pounding hard enough that the sheriff would be able to see it through her T-shirt, Robin forced her breathing to slow.

She'd done nothing wrong. Her days of being afraid were gone.

"What brings you all the way out here?" Laredo asked his friend.

"I'd like to say I'm here for the fresh goat cheese, but I met up with Ned and Augusta at the festival last night and they said your crew isn't ready."

"True. But I'll save some for you once I'm milking and Augusta gives me her recipe."

"Good to know." The sheriff shared a broad smile before jiggling Lark's bare foot. "How are you, little lady? Learning how to be a good farmhand?"

"She sure is." Laredo showed him Lark's dirty fingers. "We were just headed to the spigot to get her cleaned up. We put her handprint on the goat barn's floor."

"Nice." Kyle removed his brown felt hat, using his forearm to wipe sweat from his forehead. "Looks like it's gonna be another scorcher."

They all gravitated to the side of the barn where Laredo kept the hose.

"Don't I know it. We've been out here since seven this morning." He adjusted Lark's sun hat to keep her eyes shaded.

"If you got your foundation poured, sounds like it's time for a break. A good thing since I brought lunch."

"That was awfully nice." Laredo knelt to turn on the hose, then make quick work of washing Lark's hand. "What's the occasion?"

"Partially because Lulu had a surplus of hot dogs and pie she made for the festival, but I've also got a piece of business to run by you."

Had Chuck's father found her? Was he coming for her baby?

Robin's stomach churned to the point she feared throwing up. Why didn't Kyle get to the point? If she grabbed Lark, could she outrun both men fast enough to get Laredo's truck keys from the house, then bolt? No. At this point, even if she made it to the truck, there was no way they wouldn't catch up.

Why had she stayed?

Why hadn't she listened to the voice in her head urging her to escape by any means necessary when she'd first come to town?

"Oh, yeah?" Laredo turned off the spigot, stood, then dried Lark's tiny hand with his shirttail. "What's up?"

"Let's eat first. I've got the dogs and fixings in a cooler in my rig."

Robin noted the way Kyle didn't make eye contact. How he spoke to Laredo and even Lark, but not her. Still, he seemed friendly enough. Was she being paranoid, and he really was here to sweet-talk his friend into working another festival's recruitment booth?

"What do you think, Mary? Should I put the dogs on the grill or just boil them?"

"Excuse me?" She'd been so deep in thought that she hadn't realized Laredo had been speaking to her. Probably because he'd used her assumed name.

"I vote grill," Kyle said on the heels of a laugh. "Laredo, give Mary her baby so you can help unload the truck."

"Yessir." After passing Lark to Robin with a good-natured wink, Laredo saluted his friend.

"Smart-ass." Kyle flipped him the bird. He glanced over his shoulder at Robin. "Pardon my French. Forgot we were in the presence of ladies."

"It's okay." Her pulse slowed. Laredo had been right.

This was merely a social visit. Besides, as soon as her car was fixed, she'd be gone, safe at her grandparents' remote Ozark mountain home.

While the men unloaded a red cooler, followed by four sacks filled with buns, pies, chips and other baked goods, Robin sat on the porch swing, praying she looked calmer than she felt.

With the food unloaded into the kitchen, while the guys lit charcoal on a portable grill, Robin entered the house, tucking Lark into her playpen, then busying herself by putting perishables in the fridge. She assembled the rest along the back of the counter. Was this Lulu's way of showing Laredo her affection?

A pang tore through her at the notion of him being with another woman. But she'd sensed Lulu was a nice person. Attractive and bubbly—she'd be good for Laredo.

*Not as good as me.*

Ludicrous. Had she learned nothing from her hasty marriage? It took years to know a man well enough to determine if a woman cared to spend a lifetime with him. Not that Laredo was even suggesting such a thing. But if he had, she'd refuse.

"Doing okay?" Laredo breezed in from outside, zeroing in on the freezer.

"Sure."

"I need vodka. I'd forgotten what a pain it is lighting charcoal without lighter fluid."

"You're pouring vodka on the charcoal?"

"Worth a shot. Oh—hey, would you mind getting out a few hot dogs and setting them on a plate? I'll holler as soon we're ready for them."

"Okay..."

His mood seemed oddly jubilant. As if he hadn't a

care in the world. Meanwhile, Kyle's visit felt like one of that morning's bags of concrete hung between her shoulders. What didn't he understand about the gravity of this situation?

*Relax*, her conscience urged. *You've done nothing wrong.*

Chuck is dead and his dad is hundreds of miles away.

Her brain understood that fact, but the acid roiling in her stomach had seemed to forget.

From the bedroom, Lark fitfully cried.

Poor thing. It was past time for lunch.

"Coming," Robin said.

Moments later, Lark latched onto Robin's breast and hungrily nursed.

Robin closed her eyes and deeply exhaled. *Relax.*

If Kyle had driven all the way out here for her, surely, he would have said something by now. The fact that he'd addressed her as Mary should have also been reassuring. He didn't have a clue as to her real identity. As soon as she left, he never would.

Thank goodness Laredo hadn't slipped by addressing her by her real name.

"Mommy needs to stop being a worrywart." she whispered to her baby girl.

Aside from the occasional grunt, Lark kept right on nursing.

Robin switched her to her other breast. Usually, she enjoyed this special time with her daughter, but with Kyle outside, she felt vulnerable. As if she couldn't run even if she'd wanted. Lucky for her, thanks to Laredo's detective work with the custody research, she no longer needed to. How long would it take for her still-racing heart to get the memo?

"Mary?" Laredo was no doubt ready for the hot dogs.

"Back here," she called from her rocker, wishing she'd closed the door. "I'll be done in a minute."

"Oh—hey."

She glanced up to find him stealing all the air from the already stuffy room. He still wore his cowboy hat. His pose, leaning forward with his arms braced against the door frame, showcased his biceps and forearms and barrel chest. The man was a human tank. To have him hold her, protect her…

She drew her modesty blanket over her exposed breast.

He looked down, then up. "I, ah, was going to let you know we finally got the charcoal ready for the hot dogs, but you finish up in here and I'll handle lunch."

"Thanks."

"No problem." His crooked grin proved the human equivalent of a glass of wine. How could his wife have done such a good man wrong? Had she realized what a prize she had in him?

*You once thought the same of Chuck. Look where that misplaced trust landed you.*

Duly noted. But every fiber of her being told her this was different. Laredo was different. Such a good, kind man.

Lark took her sweet time finishing, but then promptly fell asleep.

Robin set her napping girl in the playpen, checking to make sure the room's windows were all open to allow for a cross breeze. She fastened her nursing bra, pulled down her shirt, smoothed her hair in the dresser mirror, then, before exiting, turned on the overhead fan.

As she entered the living room, Laredo eased open the porch's screen door.

Kyle trailed after him, holding the plate of grilled dogs.

"Hope you're hungry," Laredo said. "We've got enough food to host our own festival."

"Sounds good." She forced a smile.

"Kyle," Laredo asked from in front of the fridge. "What do you take on your dog?"

"The works. Mayo, ketchup, relish, mustard."

"Basically, heartburn on a bun?"

Kyle laughed while Laredo grabbed the requested condiments.

"Mary?" Still parked in front of the open fridge, Laredo looked to her. "What do you like on your hot dog?"

"I—I'll take mine dry." *Like my mouth.* Thank goodness Laredo had remembered to use her assumed name. She clasped her fingers to keep her hands from trembling.

"Lulu also sent her famous baked potato salad and coleslaw. I think there's macaroni salad and three-bean, too."

Laredo smiled and shook his head. "I'll have to make another trip. Mary, go ahead and sit down. Since you just served a meal to your peanut, how about letting me serve you."

"Th-that's nice." She stumbled backward into the nearest kitchen table chair. "Thank you."

"How can I help?" Kyle asked. "I can't have you showing me up in the manners department."

"Too late."

Robin appreciated the playful banter. It served as another much-needed reminder that her imagination was getting the better of her. Kyle truly was here for a pleasant visit. *And that business he'd wanted to discuss?* He'd no doubt taken care of it while the guys had been outside grilling. As soon as lunch was finished, he'd have a slice of pie, then be on his way.

Come morning, Robin would also say her goodbyes.

As much as the thought of leaving Laredo saddened her, this was the way it had to be. His offer to let her and Lark stay on had been beyond generous, but she owed it to herself to put space between herself and what happened with Chuck. Even if she had been emotionally unburdened, Laredo deserved better than her. She was damaged goods. Jumpy. Easily distracted. He deserved a ballsy, brassy, fun-loving spitfire like Lulu. They'd be perfect together.

So perfect that nausea swelled at the mere thought.

Laredo delivered the condiments and salads to the table, along with silverware and napkins. He handed Kyle a longneck beer and set another beside his plate. In front of Robin, he set the bottled water he knew she preferred.

While she made obligatory picks at her food, both men dug in, eating as if it had been a few days since their last meal.

"So, Mary," Kyle said between his second and third hot dogs. "Are you still planning on leaving tomorrow?"

"Yes. That is, assuming Jimmy finishes my car."

"He's a fine mechanic. We're lucky to have him. As soon as your tires are delivered, I'm sure he'll have you up and running."

"Good. I'm excited to see my family."

"Where exactly are they?"

*He's just making small talk*, she told her hammering heart. "Um, Arkansas."

"That's going to be an awfully long drive."

"Yes. But I'm up for it."

"All by your lonesome? Where's Lark's father?"

She clenched her napkin tight enough to turn her knuckles white. *Tell the truth. You've done nothing wrong.* "He's, um, no longer with us."

"I'm sorry to hear that. His name was Chuck, right?"

"Yes—I mean, no. I—"

"It's okay," Kyle said. "I know who you are."

"E-excuse me?" She tried drinking water, but her hands shook too bad to unscrew the lid.

"Kyle, what the hell?" Laredo slapped his napkin to the table. "I thought we were sharing a friendly meal? What do you think you're doing? Coming into my home, acting as if you're a guest when all along you've been waiting to—"

"Mary, I eased into this, because I wasn't even sure you were the woman I suspected. Sorry, but I needed time to assess the situation. Now that we're all on the same page, there is another matter we need to clear up."

"I have nothing to say."

"If that's how you want to play it." Kyle pressed his napkin to his lips. "Trouble is, because of all the added mess caused by the festival, I was stuck at the station until late filing paperwork. While clearing my desk, I came across a puzzling APB. It featured the face of a supposed kidnapper. The woman looked a lot like you, Mary. Only her name was Robin. Instead of dark hair, she was blonde. The bulletin gave a description of the woman's vehicle and can you hazard a guess as to what she drives?"

He took a folded sheet of paper from his chest pocket, flattened it, then set it on the table. Robin's face stared up at him.

"This is harassment." Laredo smacked his palm on the table. "Either come out and say what you're obviously here to say or get the hell off my land."

"No need to get bent out of shape," Kyle said. "But I am going to need Robin to come down to the station. Your husband's parents were understandably shocked and saddened by their son's passing. When they discovered their granddaughter was missing, they didn't take the news well. They're suing you for full custody and must have friends in high places since an emergency hearing granted them temporary full rights."

"How can that be? Lark's my child."

"That may well be, but as grandparents—especially in California—they also have rights. When you failed to show for the hearing, a warrant was issued for your arrest."

*"What?"* She felt hot-dizzy-sick.

"I'm afraid I'm going to have to take you in. As for Lark, a child welfare agent will transport her to your in-law's where she'll stay until you get this sorted out."

"No, no, no…" A low anguished sob bubbled from inside her. "I'm still breastfeeding. Lark and I can't be apart."

"I'm sorry," he said. Standing, he removed cuffs from his tool belt. "Robin Pierpont, for failure to appear at the emergency custody hearing of minor child, Lark Pierpont, I'm serving you with a felony contempt warrant. Consider yourself under arrest."

"Oh, come on." Laredo stood between her and Kyle. "You can't be serious. Clearly, this is nothing more than a petty act of grief-motivated revenge on the part of the deceased's parents."

"That may well be," Kyle said, "but that's got to be officially determined by folks way above my pay grade. All I know is that your new friend is a wanted criminal. I wouldn't be doing my job if I didn't take her in."

"Let her stay the night here. You have my word I'll bring her and Lark in first thing in the morning."

"No can do. She's already proven to be a flight risk."

"I promise I won't go." Hot, messy tears trailed down her cheeks. "Please, don't do this. I've already been through so much."

"I'm sorry." Kyle fastened the cuffs back onto his tool belt. "If you agree to come peaceably, we'll dispense with the cuffs and I'll see about getting you an expedited bail hearing. The one thing I can't do is let you keep your daughter. Until returning her to her grandparents, she's officially a ward of the state."

# *Chapter 11*

"Let's go," Kyle said to Robin. "I'll make your processing as painless as possible."

"You call essentially ripping my innocent child from her mother painless?" In a mad dash for the bedroom, she charged around the sheriff.

Seconds later, the bedroom door slammed.

"This is why I needed cuffs." Kyle sighed. "Some days I really hate my job."

"You're an ass. Would it kill you to look away? Do you know she still has bruises from the last time her dead bastard ex used her for a punching bag?" Laredo couldn't escape the truth that this mess could somehow be his fault. If he hadn't helped Kyle at the booth, if the sheriff hadn't had extra time to see Robin, maybe none of this would now be happening.

"If I were to look away, then I'm on the same level as the criminals I lock behind bars."

"Keep telling yourself that when a woman who's already been through more than enough physical and mental pain now has to endure the added agony of handing over her baby." Laredo abandoned Kyle in favor of helping Robin.

"Have her out here in five or we're doing this my way."

"Screw you. Make this any harder on her and you can arrest me, too."

"Laredo…"

Laredo didn't waste his time looking back.

Facing Robin's closed bedroom door, he knocked. When there was no reply, whether she wanted to see him or not, he entered the room only to find himself alone.

A window screen had been removed.

Gauzy curtains writhed in the light breeze.

*Shit.* Kyle would lose his mind.

Knowing she couldn't have gone far, Laredo returned to the kitchen. "She's packing. But give her ten minutes. Babies have a ton of gear."

"Thanks for talking her down. While you two get loaded, I'll put up the lunch leftovers. You probably won't feel like cooking once you get home."

"You think?" Laredo ducked back into the bedroom, closing the door behind him before jogging to the window. He crouched to exit, took a moment to plan his next move. Robin's boot prints might as well have left a neon trail in the soft, sandy soil. He followed them up and over the smallish hill behind his house. The afternoon heat beat him like a fist. Robin and the baby wouldn't last long without sun protection and gallons of water.

They had neither.

Compounding their trouble, how long until Kyle caught on to the fact that he'd been duped?

Laredo cupped his hands to his mouth. "Robin!"

When she failed to reply, he kept to her trail. A hundred yards later, Lark's pitiful cries carried on the hot, dry wind.

"Robin, stop!" When she kept walking, laden with two diaper bags, he jogged to meet her. "What are you doing other than deliberately trying to piss off Kyle?"

"He's not taking my baby."

"I won't let him. We'll think of a way. But to get him on our side, we have to at least pretend to play by his rules. Running is going to confirm his assumption that you're a flight risk."

"I am." She was still walking. "Chuck hurt me enough for two lifetimes. Now, he's hitting me from his grave. I'm done."

"I understand, but, babe, where the hell do you think you're going to go? I mean think about it. Kyle's SUV has four-wheel drive. Your tracks are easy to follow. He'll have you cuffed and in the back seat of his ride in five minutes. Even if you somehow escaped him, what then? The nearest natural water source is a good twenty miles from here. Are you prepared to hike all that way while carrying Lark and her gear without food or drink?"

"Please leave me alone. I never asked for your help or advice."

The harsh sound of a car door slamming rode on the wind.

Robin's gaze widened. "Help me hide. We can't let him find my baby."

Lark must have sensed her mother's panic. Her half-hearted complaints escalated to wails.

From back at the house a powerful engine revved.

Not even a full minute later, Kyle parked his vehicle

twenty feet from them, killed the motor, then climbed out. "What the hell? You two are forcing my hand."

"You can't take her!" Robin had grown as hysterical as the baby. "I won't let you!"

"Okay, look…" Kyle removed his hat, fanning himself with it. "This is a lousy situation for all concerned. I'm not the bad guy—just doing my job. Laredo, deliver mother and child to the station no later than six tonight. If you don't show, I'll issue a warrant for your arrest. Robin, I'm sorry for what your former husband put you through. I just received word that your in-laws are on their way. You have my word that your child will never leave your arms until you meet with them. Hopefully, once they see you being reasonable, you'll reach an amicable agreement. Sound like a plan?"

Laredo said, "I'll have them both there."

"Four hours." Kyle angled toward his SUV. "Don't let me down. The last thing I want is for this to turn any uglier."

"Agreed."

When only the dust from the sheriff's exit remained, Laredo turned to Robin. "We should get Lark out of this heat."

"I know." Head bowed, she turned for the house.

"Let me take the bags." As defeated as Robin looked with her too-thin frame, red-rimmed eyes and slumped shoulders, Laredo wished she'd let him carry her baby, too, but he assumed there was no way she'd let Lark go.

"I'm sorry," she said halfway back to the house. "For a minute I was out of my mind with terror. It felt like Chuck was alive again, pummeling me with a torture far worse than physical pain."

"I get it." Of course, he didn't. Never could.

"You're probably wondering why I never told police or any of our friends and family about the abuse."

"The thought did cross my mind."

"I have pictures in a safe-deposit box. He said if I ever used them, he'd kill me and Lark. Or take her away, making sure I never saw her again. He had the financial means to make good on that promise. I couldn't take the chance he would."

"Bastard. How did you end up with a guy like that? Weren't there signs?"

"In hindsight. But initially, he was charming. His desire to be with me. To take care of me. I loved him so much. How could a man I adored hurt me? The romance was such a whirlwind that I never saw signs that should have been red flags." She told him about her ex's possessive streak. How he'd always wanted to know her location. Keeping her all to himself—not wanting her to take a job or even have friends under the guise of them needing to spend more time together. "When you told me he was gone and I wasn't to blame, I took it as a sign that my life was finally back on the right course. Now? I'm not sure what to do? How will I fight Chuck's parents? They have the financial resources—connections—needed to work the legal system in their favor."

They'd reached the house. From behind, it looked more run-down than the front. Until now, Laredo had never felt strapped for cash or lacking in finances. He had a comfortable amount of savings from his years of service, but no way was it enough to launch a full-scale custody war against an enemy he'd never met.

He wanted—*needed*—to help Robin and her baby. But why? What was it about her that almost made him think that as long as they were together, running might be the best action?

Lord… He sounded as insane as her abusive ex.

“Sorry about your broken window screen,” she said.

“That’s the least of my problems.” They rounded the house to enter through the front door. True to his word, Kyle’s SUV was no longer in the drive, and he’d cleaned the kitchen from the mess made by lunch.

“You do realize—” she sat on the sofa, cradling her baby extra close “—Lark and I aren’t your responsibility. I never meant for any of my troubles to land on your doorstep. Since I don’t want you driving home in the dark, please take me to the police station as soon as I pack the rest of Lark’s stuff.”

“If that’s what you want.” That was it—the reason Robin and her daughter had become his top priorities. Her reminder about him not driving in the dark carried along with it the realization that for the first time since his injury, he cared more about someone else’s issues than his own. That felt good. Being back on the giving side of charity. “But I won’t leave you until this is done.”

“You’re being ridiculous. This could take months to be settled. You’ve only known me a few days.”

*I’ve always known you.* There it was—the inexplicable truth. The scent of her hair, her breath, the feel of her curves pressed against him. The way she’d made him feel safe enough to break down last night in the truck. The way she now made him feel built back up. As if he could tackle any obstacle if only to make her smile.

*You do know you’re sounding delusional?* His conscience had never been a fan of sentimentality. He didn’t do greeting cards or chick flicks. He’d sure never analyzed his *feels*.

While he'd been standing with his back pressed to the closed door, she'd left the sofa and headed for her room. She was right in her statement that once he dropped her at the station, his part in this was technically done. He'd drive away and never see her again.

*Your soul will never stop seeing her.*

And there it was—this softer, unfamiliar side of himself he'd never known. Until now, he'd never wanted to know. But that new voice spoke truth. If he dumped Robin and never looked back, how many regrets would he harbor? How many nights would he wake in a cold sweat, fearing what had become of her? Granted, he ultimately might not be able to help her win custody, but he damn well needed to try.

Robin stared past the dusty view beyond the passenger-side window of Laredo's truck. The once vibrant high desert plains that had enthralled her with rolling hills dotted with cacti and soaring coppery-toned mesas now seemed lifeless and bleak—or maybe that was her heart?

She made a quick call to her grandparents before leaving to turn herself in. They'd wanted to fly out right away, but unsure if this custody issue would take days, weeks or months to clear, she'd begged them to stay put. But her grandparents were making plans to fly in, anyway.

"How are you holding up?" From behind the wheel, Laredo glanced her way.

"Great..." She swiped more tears that hadn't stopped since Kyle first pulled out his cuffs. "I've always wanted more time to read."

"You'll barely be in long enough for Kyle to read you your rights."

"From your lips to God's ears."

They drove the rest of the way in silence. How strange that one day earlier the mood had been jubilant. Now, morose. She never took her hand from Lark's chubby tummy. With luck, she was too young for their separation to leave a lasting emotional toll. Hopefully, Chuck's parents would realize the gravity of their mistake. She'd never shared as close of a relationship as she would have liked with them, but it had never been combatant until after the divorce. She could only imagine what their son told them about her.

When they saw photographic proof of the physical damage he'd done, would they back down? Or somehow try spinning her evidence on the grounds that she hadn't provided it sooner? There were too many variables to count, which only made her stomach hurt more.

"Everything's going to be okay." After turning onto the highway leading toward town, Laredo reached for her hand.

She clung to him like a lifeline, absorbing his strength.

They passed the truck stop where her luck had irrevocably changed. First, for the better in meeting Laredo and her other new friends. But she now felt trapped in her darkest hour.

"Bet you regret ever having saved me." Her voice barely rose above the motor.

"Never." He flashed the smile that never failed to warm her. "Given a similar situation, I'd do it again."

Not for the first time, her mind drifted to how different her life may have turned out had she met a man as good as Laredo before Chuck. Her life would be simple. Easy. Tending the garden and chickens and goats. Spending long days under the sun and nights cozied up in his sweet little house, sharing dinner, playing cards, sitting on the front porch swing, gazing up at the stars.

A beautiful dream that would never come true.

When he pulled the truck into the police station lot, she thought she'd be okay, but she couldn't have been more wrong. Her skin turned hot and then cold. Her hands trembled so hard she feared taking Lark from her carrier.

Laredo parked.

He turned off the engine and exited his side of the vehicle to open her door. "Everything's going to be fine," he assured her.

She wished she believed him.

Kyle had given them a deadline of 6:00 p.m. Since the dashboard clock had read 4:47 that left plenty of time for Laredo to get safely home. "Please leave. I don't want you driving in the dark."

"Not a chance. Like I already told you, I'm not going anywhere. If I don't get out in time to make the drive, I'll grab a motel room."

A fresh onslaught of tears stung her eyes. "Thank you."

"No problem." He held out his hand to her. "You seem a little shaky. Want me to carry the peanut?"

"Please. I'll get the diaper bag."

"What about everything else?"

"Guess we can leave it for now?"

"Sounds like a plan." He unfastened Lark's safety harness, then scooped her into his arms. Robin fed her right before they'd left the house, so thankfully she was still full and sleepy.

The sheriff's station was a depressing rectangular, whitewashed building constructed of cement blocks with a green metal roof. The only concession to landscaping were a trio of yucca plants fighting for survival in a rock flower bed that held more weeds and cigarette butts than beauty.

"Breathe," he reminded her on the short walk to the entry. "Everything's going to be okay."

"You've already told me."

"It bears repeating."

Unable to speak past the knot lodged in her throat, she nodded.

He opened the right side of a pair of double doors, gesturing for Robin to enter. She would have preferred he go first, but since this was her mess, she supposed it made sense for her to take the lead.

The station proved as bleak and uninviting on the inside as it had outside. The only redeeming quality in the reception area's cramped space was the artificially cooled air.

"Hey, Laredo." A heavyset female clerk manned a built-in reception desk. She wore the same tan uniform as the sheriff without the hat. Long salt-and-pepper hair had been styled in a low side ponytail. "Kyle told me he was expecting you and a friend. Take the door on your right and I'll buzz you through."

"Thanks, Helen."

The clerk's sympathetic gaze made Robin think she knew her sad story.

A buzz sounded.

Laredo pushed open an oversize steel door that led to the station's inner workings. An open area held four unoccupied desks, a long bench with pipe dividers she assumed was for attaching cuffs and a wall sporting five ten-by-ten cells—two of which were occupied.

She shivered.

"How are you holding up?" Laredo eased his fingers between hers, giving her a reassuring squeeze.

"Not good. Suppose they have CPR gear on standby?"

"If not, I'll run you to the clinic, although I doubt the doc is in this late on a Sunday afternoon."

"Perfect." She forced a smile.

Laredo must have been here before, as he led her down a hall lined with offices and two glass-walled conference rooms. At the hall's end were two private offices. One was empty with the door open and lights out. In the other, Kyle sat behind a desk cluttered with haphazard files, fast-food wrappers and six open cans of energy drinks. A dead potted ivy graced the corner.

"Oh, hey." He pushed back his chair and stood. "You're early."

"Let's get on with this." Laredo's voice had never held such a somber tone. Robin didn't like being the cause. "We all know we're not here for a social call."

"Have a seat." He gestured to the two blue vinyl guest chairs facing his desk. "Sorry about the mess. I'm still chasing my tail after the festival. It's fun, but a little crazy." He tossed the apparently empty cans in a recycle bin, then the wrappers in the trash. Back in his chair, he said, "Robin, I'm not sure if this will make you feel better or worse, but your mother- and father-in-law's attorney called to let me know they've landed in Grand Junction. Since I'm assuming by you voluntarily coming in that means you agree to amicably transfer temporary custody, they've consented to dropping all charges."

"That's great," Laredo said. He still held her hand. She wasn't sure what she'd do if he ever let go.

Sure. The situation couldn't be more perfect. How magnanimous of the Pierponts to rip her still-breastfeeding infant from her arms. "H-how long will it take for a judge to hear my case?"

"You need to find a lawyer," Kyle said. "From there, I'm guessing this can be resolved with mediation. Considering your daughter's age, I'm sure a judge will want this resolved as soon as possible."

"Then I'll have to return to California?" Robin couldn't bear returning to her ransacked apartment—especially not without her daughter.

"Yes." Kyle shuffled papers on his desk. "Also, after the hit-and-run, a concerned neighbor entered your apartment." He consulted his file. "She said she had a key and was worried about your well-being. She told police the place was in pretty bad shape—busted furniture. A whole lot of personal property damage. A little blood. I'm presuming yours?"

Trying so incredibly hard not to cry, Robin nodded.

"For what it's worth, that fact should work in your favor."

"I would damn well hope so," Laredo mumbled under his breath.

"Look, guys..." Kyle sighed. "None of this is making my day. I'm just glad charges have been dropped. As soon as the Pierponts take custody, Robin, you're free to go."

A strangled laugh bubbled from deep in her throat. "Great."

Laredo squeezed her hand. "We'll follow them back to their bat cave. Where do they live?"

"Malibu. Their horses have sweeping Pacific views. My apartment is twenty minutes from their house. But like I said before, this has nothing to do with you."

A handheld radio on Kyle's desk squawked. He snatched it before standing. "I've got to handle this. You two stay put."

Once he was gone, shutting the door behind him, Robin lost her resolve not to break down.

"W-why are they doing this?" she asked on the heels of a sob. "If they truly love their granddaughter, this is hardly the way to show it."

"Grief does strange things to people. If they didn't know their son repeatedly hurt you, they've probably made you the villain. Once they see your evidence, they'll have no option but to recognize their son for what he was—a monster." He bowed his head. "I hate even bringing this up, but do you have a lawyer?"

She nodded. "Marjorie. After handling my divorce, we became friends. I should probably call right away?"

"Absolutely."

# Chapter 12

Robin talked to her attorney for an hour. An emergency custody mediation session was already in the works.

While she now nursed Lark in the station break room, Laredo paced the hall. One of the fluorescent bulbs flickered. Two more were burned out, lending the place a nerve-racking psych-ward vibe.

Kyle emerged from his office. "Just got off the phone with the Pierponts' lawyer. They're about fifteen minutes out."

"Lord..." Laredo raked his hand through his too-long hair.

"Back when Robin said this has nothing to do with you, she was right. I'll get her a room at Sarah's for tonight. Jimmy will fix her car in the morning, then she can be on her way to California to find a lawyer and regain custody of her daughter."

"You know this is BS." Arms crossed, Laredo stared out the window at the hall's end. They'd been at the station long enough that twilight had crept in. He used to enjoy sunsets. Now, they reminded him how useless he was in the dark. He wanted to drive Robin to her California home but couldn't. The fact made him feel like half a man. "You have no business separating a mother from her child."

"For the last time—" Kyle slapped his hand against the nearest wall "—I'm doing my job. Nothing more. As for what you're doing, charging in like this woman's protector after knowing her only a few days?" He shook his head. "It's not normal. Even Lulu thinks—"

"You want to know why I'm up to my neck in this? Because it feels damned good being needed."

"From where I'm standing, looks more like you're being used. If you're seriously considering riding this train all the way to its last stop, you could be looking at a year or more. Are you honestly prepared to waste the next year of your life on a woman you barely know?"

Laredo squeezed his hands into fists. "God, I'd love to punch that pompous look right off your ugly face."

"Go for it. I won't even charge you for assaulting an officer. All I'm asking is that you take a step back to truly think about the ramifications of following this woman to California. You've already had one woman destroy your life with lies. Why would you want another?"

"You've got this all wrong. Robin's a good person. The only reason she lied about her name and situation was to protect her daughter. Can you fault her for that?"

"If it hurts you, yes." The sheriff turned his back on Laredo to return to his office. "Mark my words, friend, might not be today or tomorrow, but eventually, this woman and her issues will annihilate you."

Laredo fought his every inner demon not to chase after Kyle to give him that punch he'd been itching to land. But what good would that do? The last thing Robin needed was to find him settling a score with violence—especially, since logically, Kyle's speech made sense. Where his words didn't compute was in that tight spot centered in his chest. The place he'd forgotten he even had—where his compassion and need for purpose had gone to hide.

Bottom line—Robin needed him, and Laredo had unknowingly craved being needed. Where was the harm in both helping each other fulfill those needs?

"I love you so much," Robin whispered to her baby girl who stared up at her while nursing. "We're going to be apart for a little while, but I promise it won't be long. Once we're back together, we'll go to your great-grandma and grandpa's house in Arkansas." A pang tightened Robin's belly at the thought of leaving Laredo. He'd been sweet and kind and supportive during a time when she'd believed herself alone.

A knock sounded on the break room door.

She glanced up to find Laredo leaning through the partially open entry.

"They're here."

"Okay. Thanks."

A few minutes later when Lark finished, Robin refastened her nursing bra and pulled down her blouse. Nerves brought on a sudden, violent round of shivers. This couldn't be happening. But it was. She had no choice but to pull herself together.

"How are you holding up?" Laredo asked when she exited the break room, cradling Lark.

"About as well as can be expected."

"Yeah. Anyway..." He tapped the metal door frame. "If you're ready, everyone's waiting."

She nodded.

Tears stung her eyes. A knot the size of Lark's favorite teething pig lurked at the back of her throat. This couldn't be happening. How had she gotten to this place?

*Cowardice.*

The first time Chuck kicked her awake that chilly October morning to drill her as to why they'd run out of coffee, she should have told her friends and grandparents and his parents—anyone who'd listen. She should have insisted on counseling.

Why had she helped Chuck hide the monster inside?

If only there was an easy answer.

"I'm sorry," she whispered to her wide-eyed child. "So very sorry. Mommy thought she could fix Daddy—make him nice for you. But all she did was end up making a bigger mess of both of our lives." She breathed in her daughter's precious scent. The lotion. The baby shampoo. A faint trace of the detergent Laredo favored. Not knowing how long she and Lark would be apart, she had to make this memory last a good long while.

Drawing on a long-buried source of strength, she forced a deep breath in preparation for her life's biggest battle.

Raised voices greeted her at the end of the short hall.

In response, Robin tightened her hold on Lark.

*"I demand to see my granddaughter."* She recognized the voice. Chuck's father—William. *"I've already lost my son to this monster. I refuse to lose my granddaugh-*

*ter, as well."* How odd that he thought her to be the monster when all along it had been his son. How would he take that news? How long after learning the truth would it take him to realize the gravity of the horrible mistake he was making in separating a mother from her child?

*"William..."* Chuck's mom. Charlotte. She and Robin used to lunch. Before the forced isolation, Robin considered her mother-in-law to be a friend. "There's no need to make this situation any more volatile. Robin brought the baby of her own free will. That must mean something. That she's willing to cooperate."

"I am." Having squared her shoulders, holding on to Lark for dear life, Robin exited the hall to enter the station's bullpen. Her ex in-laws stood alongside two suit-wearing men she assumed to be their legal team. A third man also wore a suit, but rather than study documents, he stood to the side, seeming to take it all in. Security?

Judging by the way Laredo had adopted much the same pose, Robin assumed she was right.

"Robin..." Charlotte held out her arms as if looking for a hug, but then noticed her daughter-in-law's dark expression and opted to instead step back. "I realize this must seem extreme, but please try seeing this from our point of view."

"Your point of view?" Laredo snorted. "Are you aware your son repeatedly beat her? She wasn't running to take your grandchild from you, but to save her life. Another thing—Lark is still breastfeeding. What kind of grandparents tear a child away from her loving mother at such a tender stage?"

"Who are you?" William stepped forward, hands fisted. Did he hit, too? Had he been the one who Chuck learned it from?

"I'm the man who stepped up for your daughter-in-law as opposed to your son who drove her away."

"Take Lark." After releasing an exasperated sigh, William nodded to his wife. "I can't handle one more second of this blasphemy against our dead son."

"Please don't do this." Robin would have rather withstood another fifty years of Chuck's beatings than this one impossible separation.

"Try to understand..." Charlotte reached for Robin's daughter. "We've already lost our son. We can't lose our granddaughter, too."

"But until William threatened to take her, I never would have kept her from you. You've always been free to visit as often as you'd like. I'm sorry. I was scared. I made a mistake. Please, at least give me the chance to make this right."

Charlotte looked to her husband. "Robin does raise valid points. And she is still breastfeeding."

"Take the baby and let's go." William nodded toward his legal team and security thug. "Is the paperwork in order?"

"Yessir," said the lawyer wearing a red power tie.

"Give her to me." Robin's father-in-law held out his arms.

"I—I can't..." Robin's eyes welled to the point that her world blurred. Had anyone else found it odd that neither of Chuck's parents rebuked her allegations of their son's abuse?

"Robin..." The sheriff approached. "Let's not make this worse than it already is. You'll have your day in court."

Sniffing back tears, Robin nodded, then turned to

her mother-in-law. “I— If I follow you home, will you at least feed her my milk?”

Charlotte nodded.

Robin reluctantly passed her daughter into her mother-in-law’s waiting arms. As alert as Lark was, Robin expected a fuss, but the infant settled into her grandmother’s gentle hold. Small consolation, but better than if she’d have given her to William and she’d started screaming.

“Are we good to go?” the attorney with the red tie asked Kyle.

After sorting through a pile of signed documents—Robin had already completed her share—Kyle nodded.

“Good.” William clapped to signal to his three-man crew.

The sudden noise jolted Lark from exploration of Charlotte’s pearls. As if realizing she wasn’t sure who held her, Lark pitched a full-blown tantrum.

Despite Charlotte’s best attempts to calm her screaming granddaughter, Lark spotted Robin and reached for her, pinching her tiny chubby fingers.

“I-if you’ll wait,” Robin said, “I have all of her gear. Her favorite toys and fuzzy blanket and diaper bag. Her portable playpen and—”

“We have everything she may need and more.” William turned his back on Robin, seemingly oblivious to her and his terrified granddaughter.

Lark’s every wail tore at Robin’s heart.

More than anything, she wanted to drag her child from Charlotte’s hold, but according to her lawyer that would only compound her already complex legal issues. And so she used every shred of willpower to keep her feet rooted to the linoleum floor. Days from now, this awful night would be behind her. Lark would once again be her own.

Laredo slipped his arm around her trembling shoulders, drawing her close.

"I'll be right behind you," Robin said above her daughter's wails as her in-laws and their entourage veered toward the station door. "M-Mommy loves you, my little chicken. I love you so very much..."

That last part didn't matter. Her beloved daughter had already been carried out the door.

"We have to go after them. Hurry. *Now.*"

"Babe..." Laredo would have given anything to be capable of driving all night and into the next morning for the heartbroken single mom, but they both knew his situation with the dark and she was in no shape to safely drive. "For tonight, let's grab a room at Sarah's. First thing in the morning, we'll head out."

"No. *Now.*" Desperation laced her voice with high-pitched hysteria. "I'll drive. I'm good." After using the backs of her hands to swipe tears from her cheeks, she took a tissue from the desk she stood beside to blow her nose. "See? All better..."

Her tears began anew.

"Head on over to the motel," Kyle said. "I'll call Sarah and give her a heads-up you're coming."

"Thanks, man." Laredo shook Kyle's hand.

"No problem."

Since the city streets were well lit, Laredo felt comfortable driving Robin to the motel. Unsure where the afternoon would take them, they'd packed bags with all of Robin's and Lark's belongings. Even Laredo had packed a duffel bag in case Robin wanted him to come with her.

Laredo helped still-crying Robin into the passenger side of his truck, then climbed in beside her. Darkness had long since fallen and he'd be lying if he said his nerves weren't firing terror at the thought of even the short trek across town. Logically, he knew it was no big deal, but try telling that to the demons living deep inside him.

Ignoring the voices telling him he couldn't do it, he helped Robin fasten her seat belt, hating how Lark's safety seat still had them seated with their thighs plastered together.

"You think they have an infant carrier for Lark?"

"Of course." He started the engine. "I also think that once the initial shocks wears off, Lark will realize she's safe with her grandma and grandpa."

"Is she?" Robin took a fast-food napkin from the dash to once again blow her nose. "Not sure if you noticed, but when you mentioned Chuck having abused me, they didn't flinch. It was as if their son's abhorrent behavior didn't come as a surprise."

"I suppose it's possible." He took it easy backing out of the parking spot, then took a longer way to the motel, skipping shortcuts down side streets to stick to the main, well-lit route. "If they did know the extent of their son's violence, how could they live with themselves? Especially knowing their granddaughter was also in danger?"

She arched her head back and sighed. "I don't know. Nothing makes sense. This is all a nightmare from which I can't seem to wake."

"You will." He took her hand, gliding his fingers between hers. The sudden intimacy of her palm pressed to his calmed him. The connection. The knowing he was no longer alone. Not that they were dating or anything. But they were solid.

*Really?* His conscience butted in. *How many days have you known her? And in those days, how many times has she lied and disappointed you*?

He ignored the nagging doubt to stroke her palm with the pad of his thumb.

"Thank you." She rested her head on his shoulder. "I'm always thanking you. But back at the station—if I hadn't had you with me—I'm not sure what I would have done. Honestly?" She forced a deep breath. "I'm afraid I would have found a rear exit, stolen a cop car and driven as far and fast as I could."

"Even knowing you'd surely get caught?"

"Maybe I would have ditched the squad car in favor of a less obvious ride. The desperation to keep my baby shocked even me."

"I thought your lawyer said she'd have Lark back in your arms as soon as she arranged the emergency hearing?"

"She did. But there's such a backlog of cases that she also warned it could take a week or more for the mediation to be scheduled." She yawned. "You made the right call. I'm in no shape for an all-night drive to Malibu. I don't believe Chuck's parents would hurt Lark. And once she wakes in her nursery at their house, she'll no doubt believe she's there for a nice visit. I'm the one who's a basket case."

"With good cause."

They'd almost made it to the motel when Robin said, "You do know I don't expect you to go with me. Jimmy should have my car done tomorrow. You have your goats and chickens and the garden to look after."

"I also have great friends in Augusta and Ned. While you were talking with your lawyer, I called them to ask if they'd keep an eye on my place. They agreed—assuming I'd watch their place while they're on their Christmas anniversary cruise."

"I can't imagine them on a cruise."

"Same."

Their shared smile at the mental images of Augusta and Ned's Western-themed cruise wear brought the night much-needed levity.

Laredo parked in front of the office and was thrilled to see Sarah wasn't on duty.

A red minivan pulled in next to him.

The driver smiled and waved.

Laredo managed a sort of friendly nod. "Sit tight. I'll grab a couple rooms and be right out."

"Laredo?"

"Yeah?"

"Just get one. I can't be alone."

"Understood."

Ten minutes later, Laredo had unlocked the door to room #12, then carried in the overnight bags. He checked the tarp covering Lark's things in the pickup's bed. And then he'd run out of tasks to keep him from facing Robin's tearstained hollow expression.

When he shut the room's door, he found her seated at the edge of the bed. The only light glowed from a lamp on the nightstand beside the king-size bed.

"How are you?" he asked. "Hungry? If so, the bar a few doors down makes great burgers. It's a well-lit short walk. I can grab a couple to go."

"I couldn't eat."

"You need to keep up your strength."

"Too late. It's already gone."

"Babe..." He sighed. "I won't insult you by trying to play off what you just went through as anything beyond what it was—a nightmare. But you will get Lark back. Soon."

She nodded. "Thanks again—for everything. I don't know how I could have handled this without knowing I have at least one friend."

"You've already charmed half of Dandelion Gulch. Pretty sure you're good in a crowd wherever you go."

"Stop trying to make me feel better." She bowed her head. "At the moment, I'm not feeling good at anything. My marriage was a disaster. My child was just taken. I can't even manage to get new tires for my car." In the room's dim light, her silent tears ran like liquid silver down her pale cheeks.

"Hey..." He joined her on the bed for an awkward sideways hug. "Everything's going to be okay."

She nodded before resting her head on his shoulder. They sat that way for a few minutes connected in the physical sense, but he also warred with a far deeper sensation of having known her a lifetime. How could it have only been days? How could he feel the knifelike cut of also having lost little Lark?

He took her loss as personally as if she was his. Crazy. But there it was. As undeniable as it was unexpected.

Robin straightened, meeting his gaze with her tear-filled brown eyes. She looked sad. Defeated. He wanted to cup his hands to her cheeks, to kiss her forehead and cheeks and the tip of her button nose.

He leaned closer.

His breath caught in his throat.

His heart beat faster than when charging into enemy fire.

When he raised his right hand to cup her cheek, she leaned into his touch, closing her eyes with a barely perceptible sigh.

Had she ever been with a real man as opposed to a monster? The sort of man who would put her needs ahead of his own and always ensure she knew she was protected and happy and adored?

He leaned closer and closer, bridging the distance between them until her exhalations became his breaths. "I want to kiss you. Would that be all right?"

Eyes wide and luminous, pupils dilated, she nodded. "I need to feel something besides this crushing pain."

It had never before occurred to him to ask a woman for permission for a simple kiss, yet Robin wasn't just any woman. For what she'd survived, she deserved the extraordinary—far more than he had to give.

Summoning his every shred of strength, he inched away, swallowing the dusty rock scratching the back of his aching throat.

"W-what's wrong?" Gaze still full and teary, her brows furrowed in concern.

"Nothing." He half laughed. "Everything."

The weight of her stare was palpable, yet he couldn't bring himself to look up.

"I'm going down the road for burgers. What do you like on yours?" He stood to make his way for the door.

"Really?"

"Ketchup? Mayo? Onions? Pickles?" He knew exactly what her question meant. He was just too big of a coward to admit he wasn't enough for her—could never be enough.

"Talk to me. What was that?"

"Mustard? Tomato? Mel—the bar owner—grows his own beefsteaks on the back patio. Slices 'em thick. Delicious with extra mayo."

*"Please..."* More tears thickened her voice with questions he couldn't begin to answer.

"I'm gonna get everything. What you don't want, you can scrape off." *Like gum from the bottom of your shoe. That's what a half-blind man would be to you, Robin.* Old dirty gum. Used up. Useless. He opened the door and stepped outside.

"You're an ass!"

He pulled the door shut behind him.

Whatever she'd thrown at it hit with a thump.

# *Chapter 13*

"You ever planning on talking to me again?"

*No.* Robin clung to the edge of the motel room bed with her back to Laredo. The glowing red numbers on the nightstand's alarm clock read 1:03. Instead of sleeping, instead of preparing for the fight of her life, she'd lain there hating Laredo and staring at that damned clock.

"Look, I'm sorry." His voice barely rose above a whisper. "What happened was a mistake—what *almost* happened. I—I need you to know I'm here for you. Just not that way."

Did he not want her? Did he find her unattractive? What kind of horrible mom was she that either question mattered?

Outside, the wind howled, echoing the loneliness in her heart.

"All I wanted," she said, "was human contact. To be held."

"I understand. Hell—if all you need is a hug..." He shifted closer, spooning her with his big hand cupping her belly.

"Here you go."

"Don't touch me." She wanted to move his hand, but physically couldn't when being held against him was the only thing in her cruel world that felt right.

"You don't mean that."

"I do."

When he nestled his head into the crook of her neck, his exhale warmed her cheek. "If you did, you wouldn't let me hold you like this."

*Making my heart pound and lower parts achy with the kind of need I haven't experienced in years—if ever.*

"But it's not physical. Anyone with a soul would hold you the same."

"I'm so sick of this. Of you." Of his circular BS and the way he downplayed his heroism when her daughter could have been killed. Whether he believed it or not, what he'd done in stopping that carjacking was a big deal. As was letting her stay with him till her tires were replaced. Why couldn't he see the good in himself that she'd seen all along?

Of course, she wasn't sick of him. Nothing could be further from the truth. But she was done chasing a physical encounter that would do no more to solve her problems than eating a pint of Ben & Jerry's.

"I'm sorry you feel that way." He scooted back to his side of the bed.

Damn her body for missing him on a cellular level.

"But I'm still going with you to get Lark."

"I don't need you." *Liar.*

There was an endless pause, then, "Did you ever think I might need you?"

If only that was true.

"The thought of going back to my place without you and Lark scares me." His voice was low enough that his words barely reached her.

"What really keeps you up at night is the night—the actual dark. That fear has nothing to do with me or my child."

His heavy sigh filled the room's silence and overrode the still-howling wind.

"In the morning, if you'd please take me to my car, I think it would be best if we say our goodbyes at Jimmy's."

"I think you're right."

Sometime after the glaring red clock numbers passed 3:00 a.m., Robin finally found sleep. But it came at the price of horrible dreams in which she'd lost both her daughter and the man for whom she'd inexplicably fallen so hard.

"Guess this is it." Laredo pulled his truck into Jimmy's lot, placing it in Park before taking his cowboy hat from the dash to slap it on his head. Through the open garage doors, Robin's white Focus could be seen up on the hydraulic lift. "I'll help you unload Lark's gear."

"Thanks."

They hadn't said more than a few words since waking well after nine. He never slept that late. But the sleep had felt almost as good as waking alongside her. At some point in the night, they must have gravitated toward one another. He blamed it on the saggy mattress—not on the fact that he'd wanted—*needed*—her close.

After waking, while she'd holed up in the bathroom, he'd made a doughnut and coffee run. It was now pushing eleven—a good thing since the truck delivering her tires had already come and gone.

"Hey!" Sally used her rear to bump open Jimmy's office door. She carried two yellow watering cans. "Y'all go on to the garage. I'll just be a sec. If I left it up to Jimmy to water, these poor babies would be dead by the end of the day." Midway to her first flowerpot, she paused. "Speaking of babies, where's your sweet little girl?"

Robin opened her mouth to speak, but no words made it past the knot in her throat.

"She's visiting her grandparents," Laredo said in a breezy tone. "Wasn't that nice of them? Giving Mary a well-deserved break?"

"Sure, but I thought you were nursing." Sally set one watering pot on the concrete walk before starting on the red petunias. "Are you going to pump and dump? That's what my sister did when her baby boy spent time with our folks."

Robin nodded, clinging to the truck's hood to keep her rubbery knees from buckling out from under her. Bless Laredo for not spreading her business around the small town, but she wasn't like him. She hadn't been trained in counterintelligence. This lie was too big for her to comfortably hold.

"TMI." Grinning, Laredo held his hands over his ears. "You ladies excuse me while I talk to Jimmy about something extra manly." If Robin's knees hadn't already been weak, his flirty wink would have done the job. And that smile—filled with white teeth and the kind of good looks that in better times would have melted her heart. Now, her heart was frozen.

It was a relief when he left her to enter the garage.

"He sure is a looker." Sally fanned herself. "You're one lucky girl."

"It's not like that between us."

"Then what's with the smoldering glares? There's enough heat rising from you two to scorch my flowers."

"You might need your eyes checked." Robin managed a smile.

"Nope." Sally watered her last pot. "As a bride, I've read an awful lot of articles on falling in love. You two have undeniable chemistry. It's cute."

"I'm sorry I won't be here—" Robin needed to change the subject "—for your wedding."

"Wish you'd change your mind and stick around. It's kind of nice having a new face in town—two if you count Lark."

How wonderful staying would be. Having the luxury of her own home and friends. She'd briefly had that sort of life with Chuck. It had been a few months before he'd started to change. Or maybe he'd been a monster all along, but she'd been too naive to see the signs?

"All set." Jimmy saved the day by cutting the awkward conversation when he exited the garage with Laredo.

"Wonderful," Robin said. "How much do I owe?"

"I already took care of it." Laredo tipped his cowboy hat.

"Thank you." She wanted to point out the fact that she didn't need his help—anyone's help—but the truth was that she did. Not just financially, but in every other aspect of her messed-up life.

"Let me load Lark's gear in your trunk, then I guess you can be on your way."

"Yep..." Just like that? He seemed almost eager to

let her go. She wished she felt the same. Instead, her palms sweat and pulse hammered. In some ways, facing Chuck's parents in this custody battle would be harder than taking any beating he'd delivered. With physical violence, all she'd had to do was close her eyes and pray it would soon end. A court battle could take years of constant emotional turmoil. After all she'd already been through, this new threat seemed too much to bear.

While Laredo and Jimmy loaded Robin's car, Sally set her watering cans on a bench, then wrapped Robin in a hug.

"It's been such a pleasure meeting you. Please, don't let this be a forever goodbye. At the very least, let's connect on social media."

"Yes. That sounds good." Robin pulled away without confessing she didn't have social media accounts. The concept of never again seeing Sally or Jimmy or Augusta or Ned—most of all, Laredo—was unfathomable.

"She's all yours." Jimmy held out her keys. "Gave you an oil change and checked your belts, brakes and hoses. Oh—and a new spare. You and your baby should be good to go for thousands of miles."

"Thank you." Robin took her keys before hugging the mechanic.

"No problem. Have a safe trip."

The wall at the back of her throat only allowed her to nod.

On autopilot, incapable of looking at Laredo without completely losing what little remained of her cool, she climbed into her car's front seat. The tangible connection to her old life jerked her back to reality. The nightmare would never end. Chuck's parents would never release their last living link to their son.

Seated behind the wheel with the engine running and her seat belt fastened, Robin lowered the window for a final goodbye. "Thanks again—for everything."

While she backed the car around to face the highway, Sally and Jimmy wrapped their arms around each other and waved.

Laredo shoved his hands in his pockets. His hat's brim shadowed his expression.

With one last wave, tears flowing, Robin steered her car onto the highway, driving away from the man and friends she wanted in her future to instead reconnect with her past.

"What in the name of all that's holy are you doing?" Sally fisted her hands on her hips. "Are you really going to let her go?"

"Yup." Laredo headed for his truck. He needed a long ride with Chestnut to clear his head. He feared nothing would ever help the uncomfortable tightening in his chest.

"Stay out of it," Jimmy said to his soon-to-be wife.

"I will not. Laredo, you might have trouble finding your way in the dark, but we're standing in broad daylight, meaning you should have no problem seeing that you and *Mary* share a bond it takes some people a lifetime to find."

"I offered to go with her—multiple times. She turned me down."

"To be polite. Or maybe out of pride, but trust me, no woman in her place wants to be alone."

Laredo narrowed his gaze. "Just what do you know about her situation?"

"Enough to realize she's in for the fight of her life.

Lulu overheard Kyle talking on his cell. You and I both know Mary's God-given name is Robin. We also know she didn't willingly hand over her baby girl. Go after her. *Now*. Make her pull over. Augusta and Ned will look after your place. The only thing keeping you here is your own bullheaded pride. She needs you. And I suspect you need her."

"Damn…" Jimmy settled his arm atop Sally's shoulders. "I'm not only marrying a great cook, but a spy and shrink. All of that was news to me."

"Sal—" Laredo removed his hat to wipe sweat from his forehead. The day was already turning out to be a hot one. "I know you mean well, but I'd appreciate you staying out of my business—and Robin's."

Hat back on his head, Laredo climbed behind the wheel of his truck and started the engine.

Out the open window, Laredo said, "Thanks, Jimmy, for the rush job on those tires."

"Anytime, man."

With a backhanded wave, Laredo left the mechanic's lot.

On the highway, he had five miles to decide whether or not to make the turn for home. Sure, part of him craved once again being a hero. His truck's powerful eight-cylinder engine could easily outpace Robin's four-cylinder sedan. But what then?

She'd been clear about not wanting him to join her.

But could Sally be right about Robin not having meant what she'd said? He smacked the steering wheel with the heel of his hand. Why couldn't women come right out and say what needed to be said? If she'd wanted to kiss him that bad, why couldn't she have made the first move? Why was he left feeling like the bad guy?

Say he did chase after her, he didn't know the first thing about fighting the legal system. He was an ex-soldier turned farmer. Where was the heroism to be gained from that? What use was he to her?

*All I wanted was human contact. To be held.* Her voice rang through his head.

Such a simple request. Didn't require legal smarts or even his piss-poor night vision. He just had to be there for her. Supporting her physically and emotionally. Simple.

So why did the idea of surrendering himself feel so hard?

On her way past the truck stop, Robin knew she should top off her tank and say goodbye to Lulu, but she couldn't handle another goodbye. Losing another piece of her soul.

Getting back to Arkansas, to her grandparents, used to be her primary goal. Getting home. How, in such a short time, had this dusty town become equally as dear?

Tears started again.

She gave them an angry swipe. She was sick of crying. Of losing. When would it be her turn to win?

On and on she drove. On and on tears flowed.

Maybe she needed the emotional release. Did the reason even matter? Nothing should matter beyond getting Lark back into her arms.

She fished through her purse for a travel-sized pack of tissues, swerving just in time to avoid hitting a tumbleweed rolling across the lonely road.

Launching a new search for gum, she looked down again.

Her next glance at the road had her slamming on the

brakes to avoid hitting a buck mule deer and three does. The car protested the sudden change of speed with a violent fishtail she fought to control. The right front tire hit the blacktop's edge with enough force to pop. The car lurched still more until she managed to steer it onto the red dirt shoulder.

"Whew..." After turning off the engine, she unfastened her safety belt and leaned forward, resting her forehead against the wheel.

She glanced up to find the deer family staring from the other side of the road.

"Thanks, guys. Maybe consider calling before popping over for a visit?"

Unbelievable. After waiting all this time for new tires, after barely thirty minutes of drive time, she'd already ruined one.

She left the car to inspect the damage.

The sun's heat bore down as if she were a pushpin on the barren, corkboard-colored landscape. Equally hot wind blew stray hairs into her face.

Robin rounded the car to inspect the damage. She'd hoped it wouldn't be too bad, but found the tire shredded.

Thank goodness Jimmy gave her a spare.

She unloaded the trunk and finally reached the spare only to find there was no jack. Really? *"Really?"*

Looking to the sky, she shouted, *"What's your problem with me? What did I ever do to deserve all of this? Why can't just one thing go right?"*

As if on cue, sunlight glinted off an approaching truck's windshield.

"Thank you. Sorry for the outburst..."

Stepping to the road's edge, as the vehicle approached, she waved her arms. When it slowed, she shook her head.

No way.

No. *Freaking.* Way.

# Chapter 14

Laredo's familiar red Ford slowed and then pulled onto the shoulder behind her car.

At first, Robin was elated. Beyond relieved. But then she was annoyed with herself for yet again being in a position requiring her to be saved.

He turned off his engine and hopped out—jack in hand. "Jimmy called. He found this on the garage floor. Asked me to try catching you—just in case."

"Thanks." Was this a sign? Had she been too hasty and bullheaded in sending him away?

"I'll help you change your spare, then get you back on the road."

"I'd appreciate it."

She stood alongside him while he jacked up the car, then removed the bad tire. When his dark T-shirt grew sweat-soaked, he removed it, slinging it around his neck. The sight of his bare chest and back did funny things to her stomach. Even in this most ridiculously inappropriate place, her achy longing for him returned.

Ten minutes passed with her sitting on a boulder while he worked and she wondered what she could say to make things right between them. She'd hated leaving on rocky terms, but she'd also hated having expected his kiss only to have him back away. Why couldn't he just say what he meant? Why did he have to be so infuriating to read?

*Did you ever think I might need you?*

Last night, could he have been speaking the truth?

If he had, that changed everything. It meant she was no longer solely in the position of receiving help, but also gifting help. The notion flooded her with the sort of warmth that went far deeper than that of the overbearing sun.

"Laredo?"

"Could you hand me the wrench?" He pointed behind him.

"Here." She handed it to him. Probably now wasn't the best time for a deep conversation.

*I...need you.*

Aside from Lark or her grandparents, had she ever been needed? The notion was as invigorating as it was intoxicating. It reminded her that as long as she was alive, hope for a better future for herself and her daughter was still alive. Maybe instead of wishing for Laredo to be a better communicator, she needed to be a better listener.

"All done." He rocked back on his heels.

"Thanks again."

"It was no big deal." He used his T-shirt to wipe sweat-glistening abs and pecs. Dear Lord…

*Focus.*

"You're good to go," he said.

*Apologize for being so snippy over an almost-kiss. Ask him to go with you. To stay with you.*

He gathered his few tools that lay scattered on the hard-packed red dirt.

"Laredo…"

"I need to get back to my goats and chickens." He held out his hand for her to shake. "It's been a pleasure meeting you. I sincerely hope everything goes well for you in court."

*"Laredo..."*

"Goodbye, Robin. Hope the rest of your journey is uneventful and safe." He dumped his tools into a box in the truck's bed.

*Tell him! Tell him you need him, too!*

She wanted to, but the words refused to come.

He opened the driver's-side door with a screech. Climbed behind the wheel. Started the engine.

Say something! *Anything!*

"L-last night…"

He closed his door with a slam.

"Last night I was wrong, and you were right."

"Let's not do this."

"Listen—about that kiss. You were right, we shouldn't take our friendship to a physical level. But you said you need me, and I need you, too. I'm tired of being alone—even in my marriage, I was alone. I want you with me. I don't have a clue where any of this mess with Lark is headed or how long it will ultimately take to clear up. All I do know is that I can't be alone."

He arched his head back and sighed. He killed the engine, and the sudden silence hung between them.

The deer had long since scattered.

"I need to know—" He took off his hat, raking his fingers through sweat-dampened hair. "I need to know if it's me you need, or will anyone do?"

"You. Only you."

"Why?"

"I have no idea. That's like asking why the sky's blue. It just is."

"Actually, there's a perfectly reasonable scientific explanation for the sky being—"

Climbing onto the truck's side rail, clinging to the open window for support, she leaned into the cab, closed her eyes and kissed him. She'd aimed for his lips but landed on his whisker-stubbled chin.

"You missed…"

"Because you wouldn't stop talking…"

"Wanna try again?"

Drawing her lower lip into her mouth, she nodded.

He slipped his big hand into the hair at the base of her head, drawing her closer and closer until finally they landed against each other for a soft, gentle exploration that somewhere along the way turned hard and hungry and desperate.

"Get in here," he said when pausing for air.

She shrieked when he braced his hands beneath her arms, drawing her wriggling and laughing through the window, inching back until landing her in a not-so-graceful heap atop him.

Their kiss began anew.

The heat in the cab had grown nearly unbearable, but not as bad as her need for him. She rose up to unfasten her jeans. He helped shimmy them down. His fly was the next task for her nimble fingers and when he sprung free from boxers, she settled herself atop him, inching him in. At first, the fullness hurt, but then her body grew accustomed to his size and the age-old rhythm.

Eyes closed, she enjoyed the ride. The escape. The feeling of flying far from her every trouble.

He sliced his fingers between hers, then folded them, clasping her tighter with each new thrust.

Higher and higher she climbed in a spiraling swirl of pleasure until crying out when she came with a sudden shocking intensity.

Inside her, he stiffened when spilling his seed. "I should've used a condom."

"I shouldn't have accosted you." Relishing the feel of him still inside her, she leaned forward, kissing him again.

"True."

A red minivan slowly passed. The male driver smiled while delivering a friendly wave.

Her cheeks grew even more heated. "That could have been awkward."

"Relax. We're good. Real good."

"Not really…" Straightening, she looked to the soaked front of her pink blouse.

"What's wrong?"

"My milk released."

"Isn't that good? Less you'll have to pump?"

"Yes. But it's also embarrassing."

"Do I look like I care? When we're done here, I'll get you a fresh shirt from your suitcase. And then we need to get going."

*"We?"* There went her pulse again. Racing, hoping, praying he would ignore everything she'd said the previous night. "Does that mean you want to come?"

"I always have. You were the one who decided it wasn't a good idea."

"I was wrong—out of my mind with fear."

"And now?"

She took a moment to consider his question. "I won't even try denying that I'm still terrified of how long I may be apart from my baby girl, but I'm also equally filled with determination to get her back—no matter the cost." One more issue needed to be covered, but this one was a doozy. She forced a deep breath. "When you said you need me, did you mean it?"

"Unfortunately." He softened his answer with a smile. "It's a tough thing—admitting I'm not infallible. But there it is. The thought of you being my eyes in the dark is as comforting as eating one of your meals or listening to you sing 'Itsy Bitsy Spider' to Lark. Not to put added pressure on you, but when this whole custody thing is settled, I'd love to explore the idea of you and me becoming something..." He seemed to struggle with his next words. "Hell, I don't know. I'd like for us to become something formal. A couple. Not right away. But I want you to know my intentions toward you are honorable."

"I never thought they weren't."

"Okay. Good. Now that we've got that cleared up, we should go."

"What about your truck?"

He groaned. "Jimmy offered to pick it up. Hate to be the bearer of bad news, but I guess Kyle took a private call concerning your issues and Lulu overheard. She told Sally and Sally told Jimmy—classic small-town game of telephone. Thankfully, they got most of it right. Jimmy and Sally offered to help. They urged me to go after you, but when you said you didn't want me along for the ride, I took your words at face value."

"Well, I'm glad you came after me." She cupped Laredo's dear cheek.

"Me, too. Let me grab you a shirt, then we'll reload the trunk and get going. Think we can make it to your place by nightfall?"

"Not a chance. But it doesn't matter." She kissed him. "I'm here to help you see."

They made it to Robin's apartment just after 2:00 a.m. Once the sun dipped below the horizon, she'd taken over the driving. The thankfully well-lit Spanish-styled building with its tile roof and lush gardens sat on the outskirts of Malibu proper. This early in the morning, the only sign of life was a cat giving itself a bath on a first-floor patio table and the sprinkler system's swish.

"Home." She pulled into a carport and turned off the engine. "At least it used to be home. I'll probably move as soon as Lark's custody issue is handled."

"You okay?" He opened his door and stepped outside, anxious to stretch after the long ride.

"Not even a little bit." She forced a smile. "Being back feels wrong. Being back without Lark feels like an alternate universe."

When she rounded the car to stand beside him, he took her hand, giving it a quick squeeze. "We'll have her back in no time."

"I know."

"Want me to take a batch of Lark's gear now? Or wait?"

"Wait. I left in such a hurry, it's— Things are… Well, like Kyle said, my place is a mess."

"No worries. I once had a roommate who left a sink full of dishes for a six-month deployment. Ended up throwing them away."

"You don't understand."

"Oh—you wouldn't believe what pigs my SEAL brothers could be. We had to keep everything spick-and-span during training, but once we had our own places? They let their slob flags fly."

He breathed deeply of the moist night air. He'd forgotten how much more pleasurable California weather was than southeastern Colorado.

"Might as well get this over with." She released his hand and slung her purse over her shoulder. "Come on… Is the path lit enough for you to see?"

"Yes. Thanks." She was the only person with whom he'd ever felt comfortable enough to admit the full extent of his vision problem. He'd never dreamed it could feel good to allow someone to see his vulnerability.

He followed her down a winding brick path until they reached a flight of stairs, which they climbed, making a left at the top. Five doors down, she stopped in front of the door he assumed led to her unit.

She fit a key into the dead bolt lock. Inside the dark room, she flipped a switch for an overhead light.

"Your ex was an animal." Behind her, it had taken his eyes a moment to adjust to the sudden bright light, but once they did, he saw why she'd been cagey about the state of her abode. This was no ordinary mess, but a crime scene. A former coffee table was now in two pieces. The floor was littered with broken lamps and books. Framed family photos had the glass broken out of them. In the adjoining kitchen, all the cabinet doors were open, dishes smashed on the tile floor. On top of the dishes were canned goods and pasta, crackers and cookies and moldy bread. "It's a good thing the bastard's dead. I'd kill him."

Back in the living room, sofa cushions had been slashed. Any glass knickknacks or china figurines had been shattered.

"I'm sorry." Robin scurried into action. "Please, have a seat and try to get comfortable. I'll have this place back to shipshape in no time."

"Stop." He grabbed her upper arm. "Before doing anything, we're going to take pictures. This is more evidence to show the mediator handling your case."

"But we can't prove Chuck did this. He told me as much. He said if I ever tried using his actions against him that he'd accuse me of being crazy and doing the damage myself. He threatened to take Lark from me—or worse. Even after our divorce, I had to shut up and take the abuse. What else could I do?"

"Ask for help..." Behind him, an elderly white-haired woman stood with a bejeweled three-pronged cane.

"Mrs. Jerome. H-hello. It's late. What are you doing up?" Robin greeted the woman Laredo assumed was her neighbor.

"Heartburn. Arthritis. Constipation. Take your pick. Sleep is my biggest luxury. Now, it's your turn to answer a question. Where in the world have you been?"

"It's a long story." She cast her guest a faint smile. "Please excuse the mess. I'm afraid I left in a hurry and didn't have time to tidy."

"Stop the BS, Robin. Just because I'm an old lady doesn't mean I'm stupid. I was here the day your ex did this. His crazed hollering woke me from a much-needed nap. His equally crazy father woke me again to ask about you and Lark. He said Lark was legally his, but I'm not buying that for a second. Just tell me when and where I need to be to testify against your rat ex. He deserved for that car to smash him like the rodent he was."

"Mrs. Jerome, he wasn't that bad. I—"

"Things abused women say to try justifying inexcusable behavior." The outspoken woman turned to Laredo and held out her hand. "Jessica Jerome. Friends over sixty-five call me Jess. Otherwise, Mrs. Jerome will do."

"Yes, ma'am." He answered her firm shake with one of his own.

"What's your story?" she asked. "How come I've never seen you around?"

"I'm from a small town about twelve hours west of here. Dandelion Gulch. Heard of it?"

"Oh, sure. You folks have those chicken races. Just read about it online. You're crazy, too."

He couldn't help but laugh. "Yes, ma'am, I suppose we are."

"Good to meet you. These walls are paper-thin. If I hear so much as a peep out of either one of you, I'm calling cops."

"Yes, ma'am."

She left as suddenly as she'd appeared, closing the door behind her.

Laredo whistled. "I've met admirals who didn't have balls as big as she does."

"Tell me about it," Robin said with a teary-eyed smile. "She always called police. Every time she tried helping me, talking me into getting help, I refused. I was so afraid of losing Lark if I ever told my deepest, darkest secret. Yet here I am—Chuck's dead and I'm still terrified of him taking Lark from me."

"Shh…" He pulled her into a hug. "Everything's going to be fine. There's no way any judge or mediator would award custody to anyone but you."

"Hope you're right."

"Of course, I am." He held her till her tears subsided, then asked, "Any chance your bedroom fared better than the rest of your place?"

"Hope so…" She locked the front door, then flipped on the light switch for a short hall. At the end, she entered a room to their right, again, turning on the light switch ahead of him.

Aside from a few open dresser drawers with clothes hanging out, the bed was made with a floral spread and all tabletops were decorated with collectables and framed photos of Lark and a couple Laredo assumed was Robin's grandparents. Pale pink walls held bucolic landscape paintings and more family mementoes.

"You should let your grandma and grandpa know you made it back safe."

"I will first thing in the morning. Unlike Mrs. Jerome, they're asleep every night by nine."

He yawned. "I envy them."

"Want a quick shower before bed?"

"Are you saying I need one?" He winked.

"That T-shirt of yours has seen better days. Although…" A shy smile tugged the corners of her lips. "I have to say you looked pretty amazing with it off."

"That's not fair. When do I get to see you without a shirt?"

*"Laredo..."* Hands pressed to his chest, she bowed her head, but not before he caught her pretty blush. "You shouldn't say things like that."

"Why not? Have you forgotten that you were the one who first kissed me?"

"Come on then..." Slipping away from him, she entered the attached bath to turn on the lights before removing her clothes.

# Chapter 15

"I'm excited to see you, Grandma." Robin watched through her apartment's living room window while Laredo hauled another load of trash to the dumpster. First thing that morning, he'd gone out for heavy-duty bags—and of course, doughnuts and coffee. Lord did that man love doughnuts.

And Lord, did she love—Robin had been on the verge of thinking she may have fallen hard enough for Laredo to love him, but it was too soon. Look how fast she'd married Chuck. What she and Laredo shared was undeniably special, but for herself and most especially for Lark, she had to take their relationship slow. With her mind focused where it needed to be, she asked, "Are you sure you and Grandpa are feeling good enough to travel?"

"Absolutely. We want our day in court. No one's going

to take your daughter from you without us putting up a fight—especially not after all you've been through."

"But my lawyer hasn't even told me when we'll see a judge or a mediator. I don't see her till later this afternoon."

"When are you visiting Lark?" her grandmother asked.

"Hopefully soon. I'm waiting till nine to call Charlotte."

"Sounds good. I'll let you know when we have our flight times."

After a few more minutes' small talk, Robin ended the call. The thought of seeing her grandparents made her happy. The thought of introducing them to Laredo filled her with dread. It wasn't that she was ashamed of her feelings for him. Or maybe she was?

From her viewpoint, her soul felt as if she'd known him forever. But what would her family think of her jumping into another relationship so soon?

The door opened and in walked the object of her thoughts.

"How was your call? Everything good with your grandparents?"

"Perfect. They're flying out. They want to be here for the initial custody hearing." After averting her gaze, she added, "They also want to meet you."

"Uh oh." He closed the door. "Is that good or bad?"

"Not sure." She drew her lower lip into her mouth. "I don't want them to judge me. But how can they not when I'm judging me? This thing between us… It's been a whirlwind."

"True." He joined her on the comfy tan sofa that didn't look half bad after they'd shoved the stuffing back in before flipping over the cushions. "And you're worried that because you and Chuck married too fast, that you could also be making a mistake with me?"

How had he read her mind?

"Look..." He took her hands. "I'm not asking you to marry me—at least not yet. My own marriage was a train wreck. Nothing like yours, but it still left a plenty sour taste in my mouth. Believe me, I get where you're coming from."

"Thank you." She smiled. "Seems like I'm always thanking you."

"That's because I'm awesome. And in case you needed reminding, you have a couple of flight attendants down by the pool who weren't shy about welcoming me to their neighborhood."

"Don't even think about straying, mister." She pulled him within kissing distance by hooking her fingers over the collar of the LA Dodgers T-shirt she'd loaned him. It was an extra-large she used for a nightshirt.

"Mmm..." The feel of his lips pressed to hers filled her with hope for their future. Even better, hopefully within the hour, she'd finally be reunited with her daughter—at least for a little while. Even a short visit was better than nothing. "Not that I wouldn't love sitting here making out all day, but now that it's nine, don't you have another call to make?"

"Yes, I do." She didn't bother trying to downplay her supersized grin. "I can't wait to see my baby girl. I would have called earlier but didn't want to risk waking Charlotte. I know she sleeps late." She leaned forward, taking her cell from the oak coffee table that Laredo had reassembled with wood glue and carpentry braces.

She'd wiped her dried blood from it before he'd seen. "Eek. I'm so excited my hands are shaking."

"I don't blame you. I'll bet she'll be super excited to see you."

She placed the call to her mother-in-law, putting it on speaker.

"Robin?" Charlotte took five rings to answer. "Are you still in Colorado?"

"No. I'm at my apartment. How is Lark?"

"Good. We've started her on solids and she adores peaches. She makes the cutest little face with every bite. You really should—"

There was a muffling sound in the background, then, "Robin, this is William. My wife says the two of you made arrangements regarding the baby's feeding, but that's not going to work."

"What do you mean? I'm still breastfeeding. Her pediatrician said—"

"Interesting how you care about her doctor now, yet when you stole our granddaughter like a thief in the night, you failed to consult him then."

"I want to see my baby."

"You should have thought about that before taking her across state lines and violating your custody agreement."

"Chuck is gone. I'd assumed shared custody went away, too."

"*Gone?* He's not on an extended vacation, but *dead.* Because of you." The call ended.

*"Ohmygod."* A slow tremble worked through Robin until her entire body shivered. "Charlotte said I could visit Lark whenever I wanted. What changed?"

"Try to take deep breaths." Laredo slipped his arm

around her, drawing her close. "Everything's going to be okay."

"How?"

"What time do you see your lawyer?"

"Two this afternoon."

"Until then, let's get this place shipshape, all ready for Lark's return. You need to stay positive. Promise—everything's going to work out fine."

"What do you mean they're within their rights? Lark is my child." Laredo winced when Robin's tone took on a ring of desperation. They'd been at her lawyer's for over an hour and the news wasn't good. In fact, it was alarming enough to make him regret that morning's speech about keeping a positive attitude when he should have been prepping the single mom for battle. "I don't see how any of this is even legal."

"I assure you it is—although, barely." Marjorie leaned forward in her ergonomic desk chair. Tall and lean, with minimal makeup and her hair styled in a no-nonsense bob, she struck Laredo as being as streamlined as her office. A black desk and bookshelves were void of any decor but what he could only guess was essential case research material. The lines of the third-floor room's smooth gray walls were only interrupted by her diplomas and a panoramic ocean view. With black desk chairs and dark-stained hardwood floors, the only spot of color was a canister on her desk filled with yellow M & M's. "As an entertainment attorney, like your ex, William has friends in high places. Working in our favor is the fact that he also has enemies. I've got an emergency mediation meeting scheduled for Thursday at 8:00 a.m. My secretary will call with location details and arrange transportation for Mrs. Jerome. Bring the photo evidence we used at your divorce hearing."

"About your fee." Robin's sober expression pained him. He missed her smile. "I'm afraid I don't have—"

"No worries." Marjorie held up her hands. "I'm considering this an extension of your divorce. The fact that Chuck got off paying such a pittance when he was worth millions still chaps my hide. I didn't mention it earlier, but I'm countersuing on Lark's behalf for the entirety of her father's estate. You'd receive a monthly stipend till she turns eighteen, at which point the funds will transfer to her in time to pay for the best education a mother could hope for."

Tears filled Robin's eyes.

"No more of that." Marjorie rose, rounding her desk to wrap Robin in a hug. "We'll get your daughter back. That's a promise."

"Thank you."

Laredo helped Robin to her feet, then shook the lawyer's hand. "We appreciate your help."

"About that..." She winced, gesturing between him and Robin. "Until after the hearing, Laredo, it would be best if you lay low. Opposing council is grasping at any straw to prove Robin an unfit mother. The fact that you two have become an *item* in such a short time doesn't speak highly of Robin's character—not that I disapprove. But you both need to know your relationship could become a negative pivot point. Laredo, I don't want you anywhere near the hearing. Also, avoid any PDA. Robin, it wouldn't surprise me if William hired a PI to tail you—just waiting for an opportunity to besmirch your character."

Once they'd left the lawyer's Malibu office and had

sat through three red lights, Laredo glanced at Robin to find her staring into the traffic, her big brown eyes pooled with pending tears.

"I need to go," he said.

"What do you mean? Like you need a restroom?"

"I wish it was that simple." He laughed and shook his head. "I mean, I have no business being here. If what Marjorie said was right, my presence is only hurting you."

"Don't say that."

"You know it's true."

"I can't do this without you."

"Looks like you might have to."

She shook her head. But then with her eyes tearing, nodded. "I hate this, but I'm afraid you're right."

"I am. We're not talking forever. Just until you get Lark." He reached out to cup the crown of her head. Silent tears falling, she leaned into his touch.

The light again turned green and they finally passed through the crowded intersection. Sun sparked off the Pacific, glistening, teasing with the promise of picnics on the beach and wave surfing and sandcastles. What the endless expanse of blue didn't say was what lurked beneath. Pressure that could crush a man's skull like a melon. Impenetrable darkness. Sharks.

How did he get Robin to understand that no matter how untenable the thought may be, now was the time to swim deep. To face the darkness head-on and fight on its terms. Rules of engagement had to be followed. Strict safety protocol. How could the SEAL in him not have seen it before? The fact that for William and his legal crew, having him around must be the equivalent of chum in the water.

He'd unwittingly become the perfect bait for discrediting Robin's honor.

Whether she liked it or not, he needed to go.

"I can't believe you're here." Robin said the next day as she reached across the seaside café's table to clasp her grandmother's weathered hand. After all these years, her beauty still shone through her twinkling blue eyes. She had her hair done every Tuesday with her blond curls brushed into an upswept chignon that Robin used to tease held enough hairspray to serve as a helmet. "Thank you. You, too, Grandpa."

"Where else would we be?" her grandmother asked. "I'm just sorry to hear your lawyer doesn't feel better about your case."

"It's not that she thinks we won't win per se, just that it's not the slam dunk she'd hoped for. Chuck's parents had me arrested for kidnapping. They'd arranged for an emergency custody hearing without even letting me know. Then, when I failed to show up in court, that gave their judge friend the ammunition he needed to issue a warrant. I was lucky they dropped the charges. Pretty sure I have Charlotte to thank for that."

"I always liked her." Her grandmother sipped her iced tea, staring out at the crashing surf. "I believe she has a good heart. Her husband on the other hand…" She shook her head. "He was always a little too controlling for my taste. Wish I had seen the same signs in his son."

"To this day—" her grandfather dredged a fry through ketchup only to drop it back to his plate "—it sickens me to think I gave my blessing to your union. I'm sorry about that. You don't know how many times I've asked myself how I could have missed the signs."

"Because he didn't show any." Beneath the table, Robin pressed her palm to Laredo's thigh. He'd been zoned out through lunch—come to think of it, he'd been awfully quiet since meeting with Marjorie. "One of the things that Laredo and I bonded over was the fact that his ex-wife wasn't honest with him, either."

He cleared his throat. "If you don't mind, I'd rather not discuss Carrie."

"Of course. I didn't mean to—"

"It's okay." He squeezed her knee. "Shirley, Earl, tell me about your farm. I'm not sure if Robin mentioned it, but I've started a homestead and recently brought in goats. I'd like to make my own cheese—maybe even enough to sell at the Saturday farmers market."

"Goats can be cantankerous," Earl said. "You've gotta watch 'em like hawks." He turned to his wife. "Remember when you bought me those good-looking leather gloves for my birthday? That damned billie—think Robin named him Brad Pitt—ate them right off my hands. Was the damnedest thing. They're fast little buggers, too. Yessir, you've gotta watch 'em." He finished his iced tea and signaled the waitress for another.

Robin was thrilled for the change of topic.

Her grandmother asked, "Do we need anything special to wear to the mediation? I brought my best church dress and your grandfather's suit."

"That should be fine." Robin pushed her mostly uneaten club sandwich away. Just thinking about the custody battle stole not only her appetite, but her joy over being reunited with two of the people she held most dear.

She covered a yawn.

"You look tired," her grandmother said. "How about we go back to your place and take a nice, long nap?"

"Sounds heavenly, but I doubt I could sleep."

"Where are you staying?" her grandfather asked Laredo.

Awaiting Laredo's answer, Robin froze. Her grandparents had always been progressive. Why now were they being prudes?

"I've, ah, got a room at a motel not far from Robin's place."

"Good man. I appreciate you not taking advantage of our granddaughter."

Eye roll. *Really, Grandpa?*

"Laredo," she said, "as much as I appreciate you trying to protect my honor, I'm not going to lie when you've helped me through all of this. Grandma and Grandpa, Laredo is staying with me. We're both consenting adults and doing nothing wrong."

Her grandfather crossed his arms.

Her grandmother shook her head.

"Looks like we'd better get a room," her grandfather said. "If things are that hot and heavy, we don't want to intrude."

"Please, guys. Not that our relationship is like that, but I'm closing in on thirty. Can we keep this discussion relevant to what's really important—getting back my daughter."

With her grandparents asleep on the pullout couch in Lark's nursery, Laredo finally got a moment alone with Robin.

"That was some lunch..." He joined her on the sofa where she'd been reading the same page of a book for the past ten minutes. Not that he'd fared much better with his *LA Times* crossword.

"Tell me about it." She set her open book on her lap.

"I thought once I'd passed eighteen, I no longer needed permission to see my boyfriend."

"Is that what I am? Your boyfriend?"

She lowered her gaze. "Do you want to be?"

"I think you already know the answer to that. The real question is do I need to be?"

Sighing, she said, "Let's not get into this again. I already told you—"

"Your lawyer made a helluva valid point. At lunch, your grandparents basically echoed the same thing. Don't you see? That means something. If I truly care for you, the best way for me to show it is by letting you go."

When she started to voice her latest protest, he held up his hands.

"Let me finish. I'm not talking forever. See this as a goodwill gesture. A sign to your ex's parents that you take their concerns seriously."

"But their concerns are ridiculous—nothing more than a manufactured reason for them to keep me from my daughter."

"That may well be, but until Lark is back in your arms, do you really want to give them one more reason? I don't."

She held her hands to suddenly aching breasts.

"Need to nurse?"

Nodding, she said, "I'm behind on my schedule."

"Want me to get your pump?"

"Thanks, but I'd better do it in the bedroom. God forbid my uptight grandparents see me using such high-tech equipment on my boobs."

"Don't be hard on them. They want the best for you. Same as me. Which is why I called an Uber."

"Why?" She lurched forward. "Please tell me you're not going back to Dandelion Gulch."

"I'm not. But I am getting a room at that little inn down the road. If you need me, I'll only be a few miles away. But until Lark's home, whether you like it or not, whether it's logical or not, we both need to play by Charlotte and William's rules."

# *Chapter 16*

*"Ladies and gentlemen of the jury, have you reached a verdict?"*

*The jury foreman—an older gentleman with wavy gray hair, stood. "We have, Your Honor." He handed a folded slip of paper to a bailiff who in turn handed it to the stone-faced judge.*

*"Foreman Tubbs, when you're ready, please deliver your findings."*

*"We, the jury, find Robin Pierpont guilty of being a bad mom in the first degree. It is our recommendation that she never again be granted custody or visitation with her daughter."*

Laredo woke with a start.

For a terrifying few seconds, he couldn't see and didn't know where he was. Then it all came rushing back. The car rental. The room at the inn. Robin's latest tears.

What was he doing here?

Not just in this room, but this town?

How had he transitioned from knowing a woman for a few days to dreaming about her? To following her hundreds of miles from his home?

He needed to pee but dreaded the perilous trek to the bathroom. Why hadn't he left on a light? He knew better than to fall asleep without giving himself a lifeline should he wake before dawn. But exhaustion had claimed him before dark. And now, he needed to suck it up—his fear, his doubts, his terror that after temporarily being apart, Robin might find herself permanently better off without him.

Which would be true.

He had to let her go. But how?

And if he did manage to walk away, what then? How did he carry on with his life without her and Lark in it? His dependence on her made no sense, but when had being with any woman been a sound decision? Look what happened with Carrie. If he hung around with Robin, was he only asking for the same kind of pain?

Pushing himself upright, he managed to get onto his feet, but then stumbled over his boots. Recovering from that near-fall, he shuffled forward, heart pounding, palms sweating, feeling his way through the darkness by using the bed. Once he'd rounded the corner to the bed's foot, he continued feeling his way until hitting a wall. He remembered it served as a wing wall with the bathroom on the other side. Once he rounded that, he was home free when finding a switch.

The sudden light made him wince.

He faced himself in the mirror mounted above the sink. "You look like shit."

Beyond needing a haircut and shave, his eyes were red-rimmed, as if he'd just returned from an unusually long mission.

It felt like a lifetime since he'd used his crossbow to shoot out Robin's tires. How could it have been only days? Not even a full week.

When he viewed their relationship in those terms, he understood her lawyer's and grandparents' apprehension toward his sudden appearance in Robin's life.

What he would never understand is why every time he so much as thought about her not being in his life all the air felt sucked from his lungs.

"First, this session is being recorded. Second, I applaud both parties for agreeing to reach a decision in this matter via mediation. It is my hope that I'll reach a decision by the end of today as opposed to court rulings that can sometimes take months or even years. In the case of a minor child..."

While the mediator rambled on, Robin wiped her sweating palms on her navy-colored skirt. She'd hoped to see Lark, but during the session she'd been left with the nanny the Pierponts had hired. Knowing her daughter had been tucked into a playroom somewhere in this vast building, yet not being able to hold her, was beyond devastating.

"Mrs. Pierpont?" the mediator asked.

"Yes?" Robin and Charlotte said at the same time.

"For clarity, if neither of you object, I'll use your first names. Are you both agreeable?" The woman smiled. She seemed pleasant enough. Auburn hair tucked into a bun. Black business suit softened by a frilly white blouse and pearls.

Robin swallowed hard and then nodded.

Charlotte nodded, as well.

"Very well. Let us begin…"

Two hours passed.

After Robin's initial charges were explained, the attorneys exchanged volleys concerning her involvement—or lack thereof—in her ex-husband's death.

Each time her son's name was mentioned, Charlotte's eyes welled.

William's expression turned harder.

Marjorie slapped her palms against the table. "Could we please stay on topic? My client has been cleared of any wrongdoing regarding her late ex-husband's death. The matter at hand is whether she is a fit mother. You contend the fact that she left town so abruptly speaks volumes about her lack of sensitivity. I have the evidence and witnesses to prove Robin quite literally believed she was running for her and her baby girl's life."

"Nonsense!" William slammed the table with the heel of his hand.

"Might I remind all of you," the mediator said, "that the key to a successful mediation is to thoughtfully listen to all parties involved. Mr. Pierpont, you will have ample opportunity for rebuttal. For now, I'd appreciate you letting your daughter-in-law's attorney have the floor."

William glowered.

His two attorneys—the same two goons who had been with him the night he'd taken her baby from her—put their heads together, whispering behind their hands.

Marjorie reached into her briefcase. "Please accept Exhibits A thru S—photos of the abuse my client suffered at the hands of the deceased." She fanned the pictures across the table for all to see.

Bruising so severe on her back that her flesh had turned purple. Distinct handprints. Her badly broken arm Chuck had blamed on her falling down stairs. On and on the parade of photos marched, telling a story Robin would never fully be able to put into words.

Next came still more images of the most recent damage he'd done to her apartment.

Charlotte gasped, covering her mouth with her hands.

"All of this is ridiculous," William said. "How do we know she didn't pull these off the internet? Furthermore, the ones showing her face could have been altered. Happens all the time. And if the alleged abuse was so bad, why wasn't it addressed in divorce proceedings?"

"Because I was scared!" Robin couldn't hold in her frustration a moment longer. "Chuck said if I ever told anyone he'd kill me and Lark. I just wanted my freedom. For Lark and me to be safe. To get away from him, I would have agreed to anything, but I can't be a victim anymore."

"So now you've decided to become a liar?" William leaned back in his chair, folding his arms.

The color drained from Charlotte's face.

Marjorie said, "I would like to call our first witness."

A former housekeeper who'd signed an NDA but was no longer bound to it after Chuck's death admitted having seen and heard Mr. Pierpont repeatedly strike his wife with the seat back of a chair he'd broken.

Her personal physician said, "I pleaded with Robin to leave him. He once beat her so severely during her pregnancy that I feared for the life of her baby. As I'm bound to do by law, I notified police, but Robin refused to file charges."

"Because my son didn't do this!"

"Mr. Pierpont." The mediator stood. "One more outburst and I'll have you removed from the proceedings."

Mrs. Jerome came next, followed by Robin's grandparents. She should have told them—everything. But she'd been too afraid of the inevitable repercussions.

"I would like to close my portion of these proceedings," Marjorie said, "by reminding all present that before the unfortunate death of the Pierponts' only child, they felt my client was not only an adequate, but good mother. My client allowed liberal visitations and was present with her child for all major holidays. With this is mind, how is she now unfit to raise her infant daughter? My client has been denied her most basic rights of even breastfeeding her baby and for what? To soothe the grief-stricken egos of her former in-laws who—"

"Will someone shut her up?" William's face turned red enough that a vein popped out on his forehead.

"Mr. Pierpont." The mediator again stood. "Remember my former warning. I think this is a good place for us to pause. Let's be back in session by 1:00 p.m."

During the lunch recess, Robin called Laredo, needing to hear his voice, but he didn't pick up.

"This is going great," Marjorie said. In a park located a block from the mediation offices, they'd ordered sandwiches from a food truck and eaten—or, Robin had tried eating—at a picnic table in bright sun. "By tonight, Lark will be back with you—forever. Or at least until she meets her first boyfriend." She winked.

"Ha ha." Robin tossed her crusts to a trio of bickering wrens.

"Did we do okay?" Robin's grandmother asked.

"Perfect." Marjorie started on her pickle. "Thank you

both for coming. I feel good about firmly having established the fact that Robin felt her only option was to run."

They had another twenty minutes before they were due in the stuffy mediation room. To Robin, it felt like a cell.

She tried calling Laredo again, but had no luck.

All too soon, they'd reassembled at the table.

Her grandparents had been allowed in the room only during their testimony. For the remainder of the afternoon, they'd waited on hall benches.

The Pierponts' lead attorney stood. "While we have no wish to downplay what Robin may or may not have endured, my clients' deceased son's former lifestyle is not at issue. What we're here to decide is whether Robin is currently a fit mother. We contend that through events we may never fully understand, her judgment has been impaired to the point that she is no longer capable of raising her infant child."

Robin pressed her lips tight to keep from crying out. Tears threatened to spill.

Her chest felt tight and she clamped her sweating palms to her thighs. Was there enough air in the room? There couldn't be, since it had become a struggle to breathe.

"Mere days after her ex-husband was savagely run down by a car, Robin fled the state with the Pierponts' granddaughter. As if that wasn't egregious enough, she promptly thereafter launched an illicit affair—moving in with a man she'd known not even a full twenty-four hours. My clients contend this shows a blatant disregard for her infant daughter. For all she knew, this man could have been a serial killer, yet—"

"As opposed to a serial wife beater who repeatedly

threatened to kill his wife and daughter if she uttered so much as a whispering of the hell she was living?" Marjorie pushed onto her feet. "Let the record show the 'man' with whom my client temporarily resided is a fine, upstanding member of his community. He's a former Navy SEAL who served our country for thirteen years. He also saved my client's child from the carjacking incident which resulted in her vehicle being disabled. That's the reason why she was forced to stay in this 'man's' small town. Despite your clients' incalculable wealth, because my client is given a pittance for child support, she had no option other than to rely on the kindness of others who gave her food and shelter when her own family couldn't—or, in the case of the Pierponts—*wouldn't*."

"If the opposing council has finished her rant," William's lead attorney said in a bored tone, "I will begin introducing our own evidence. As soon as my clients discovered the whereabouts of their granddaughter and her mother, they engaged the assistance of a private investigator to ensure Robin didn't again flee. While my client never intended to catch his daughter-in-law in a compromising position, he was shocked to discover her flagrant disregard for societal norms."

He flung a pile of incriminating photos to the table. Shots of her and Laredo hugging in their room at Sarah's motel. Laredo shirtless while changing her tire. Her approaching Laredo's truck. Standing on the running board. Diving in headfirst for a kiss. Even more shots of that sordid afternoon on the highway when she and Laredo had lost themselves to temporary insanity in the cab of his truck.

How had the investigator even gotten the shots? With a telephoto lens?

Closing her eyes, back on that lonely stretch of highway, she saw the passerby smiling in his red minivan. Had that been him? Knowing he'd scored a major coup?

"In fact," the Pierponts' attorney rambled on, "Robin's lack of propriety didn't end in the town of Dandelion Gulch where she surrendered but has continued right here in our fine city."

He tossed down more photos of Laredo entering and exiting her apartment. Hugging her on her balcony. Kissing her on her living room sofa.

Never had she felt more violated.

How was this depth of privacy invasion even legal?

"In layman's terms," the lawyer continued, "my clients would prefer their granddaughter not be raised by a common whor—"

"That's it." Marjorie was again up from her seat. "Have we regressed a couple centuries in the time we've been in this room? Since when is it a crime for two consenting adults to take pleasure in each other's company? I'd also like to point out that at the time my client engaged in these alleged adult activities, her daughter was not in her care."

"Thank goodness!" William was at it again. "Who knows what went on behind closed doors. She could have offered this stranger her body in exchange for—"

"Mr. Pierpont," the mediator said, "I'm at the end of my rope with you. Please leave the room."

"I will not."

She stood. "Yes. You will." She pointed toward the door. "Out. If you don't leave under your own free will, I will have building security escort you."

He shot a look to his lawyer, who nodded.

With a put-upon huff, William exited.

"Let the record show Mr. Pierpont is now gone. He will be readmitted when I render my decision."

William's lead lawyer said, "I would now like to introduce our witness, Mr. Laredo Tucker."

*What?*

The room spun.

Was this why she hadn't been able to reach him?

He entered wearing an ill-fitting suit. Since she'd last seen him the previous day, he'd shaved and gotten a haircut.

"For the record," William's lawyer said, "Mr. Tucker is only here because he was compelled under threat of contempt upon failure to appear."

"Very well." The mediator made a note. "Mr. Tucker, please be seated and know everything you say will be recorded."

"Yes, ma'am."

William's lawyer questioned Laredo ad nauseam regarding the logistics of how she'd come to stay with him and what the sleeping arrangements had been while she and Lark stayed at his home. "Do you make a habit of having relations with random women on the side of state highways?"

"What does any of this have to do with my client's ability to raise her child?" Marjorie threw her hands in the air, slapping them onto the table. "God help us all as a race if anyone who has a child must be forever done with all sexual relations."

"Ms. Bowen," the mediator said in a low tone. "One more outburst and you will be seated in the hall alongside Mr. Pierpont."

"May I say something?" Charlotte raised her hand.

"Of course." The mediator raised her eyebrows as if surprised the woman had a voice.

"Robin, I'm terribly sorry about all of this. You have to know it wasn't my idea. When William suggested it, I thought he was mad. But then you were gone and not answering your cell. I was out of my mind with grief over losing Chuck, but even more so over what kind of man he'd become." She bowed her head. "You'll never know how deeply saddened it makes me to learn he turned out just like his father—only William eventually sought help to break his cycle of violence. He hasn't so much as raised his voice at me in over twenty-five years. Not that I'm excusing Chuck's actions, but he learned them through watching his father abuse me."

The mediator passed Charlotte a tissue box.

"Robin," Charlotte continued, "let's put all of this ugliness behind us. You know we have a lovely guest cottage. We can raise Lark together. All you have to do is agree and I'll gladly sign over full custody. Please, say you'll bring Lark to live on our ranch." She looked to Laredo. "You and your baby girl will want for nothing. She'll grow up around horses with servants and nannies. First-class travel and private schools. Of course, you'll also be well-provided for. A monthly stipend if you'd like—certainly enough that you'd feel comfortable staying home to be a full-time mom."

"Let me get this straight." The mediator leaned forward. "Assuming your ex-daughter-in-law agrees to reside with you at your place of residence, you'll drop this entire proceeding?"

"Yes." Charlotte vigorously nodded.

Robin's heart swelled with hope. Her initial thought was an emphatic yes. But then she looked to Laredo.

And realized the full gravity of the awful position she suddenly faced.

Charlotte was essentially asking her to choose.

Laredo.

Or her daughter.

# Chapter 17

"I have a question."

All eyes turned to Laredo, whose heart hadn't pounded so hard and fast since his last time in combat.

"Yes, Mr. Tucker?" The mediator jotted a notation on her mountain of papers.

"Would it be cool for me to officially remove myself from this equation?"

"Excuse me?" The mediator furrowed her brow. "I don't understand."

"In plain English, I want no further association with the younger Mrs. Pierpont. Consider us broken up." Getting the words past his throat was akin to puking broken glass. Only just now—upon watching Robin struggle with her decision to choose him or her daughter—did he realize that as asinine as it sounded even to his own heart, he hadn't just fallen for her and Lark, but he loved them. Because of that love, he had to let both go. Charlotte's offer had been more than generous. No way should Robin even consider refusing—certainly not for him. "I mean, it's been fun and everything, but I haven't lived to my ripe old age not to realize when I'm in over my head." Though he strove for a devil-may-care asshole's tone, this heartless speech might literally kill him—that is, if his one look at Robin's pained expression didn't. He forced his hands up in the classic surrender position. "Robin, it's been fun, but peace out. This is too much drama for me."

Her tearing eyes asked, *What are you doing? I thought what we shared was real?*

*It is—was,* he longed to convey. But how could he when he was trying to be noble by making this awful decision for her? Besides, she could do so much better than getting herself tied down to a blind man who had little more to his name than a run-down homestead and a horse, a few goats and some chickens.

He rose from his seat and, after gracing the mediator with a mocking bow, said, "Y'all enjoy the rest of your day. I need a beer and to ditch this monkey suit."

On his way out of the room, he heard a chair scrape back. Robin's?

She asked, "Is it all right if I go after him?"

"No," he heard her lawyer say. "There's a more than generous offer on the table and as your counsel, I'd advise you to take the deal. There are plenty of men in the sea. Clearly, you don't want that one."

On that sour-ass note, Laredo exited the room, closing the door firmly behind him—not just on the legal proceedings, but on any chance he may have had of him and Robin and Lark forming their own little family.

* * *

*But I do want him*, Robin's heart cried.

"For my own clarification," Marjorie said to Charlotte, "you will be amenable to Robin eventually dating? Visiting her family in Arkansas? Eventually returning to the career she found fulfilling?"

"Of course." Charlotte turned to her former daughter-in-law. "Robin, more than anything, I wish you'd come to me about the abuse. When I heard about the divorce, I had my suspicions, but William urged me to stay out of you and our son's troubles. Now, I just want the ugliness to go away." She was once again crying. "I want us to be a family. I'll never again have a son, but with you, I could have a daughter and granddaughter."

How was any of this happening? Had she fallen into the *Twilight Zone*?

Laredo's bad-boyfriend act had been stupid-easy to see through. Which meant he was falling on his sword for her.

*I need you.*

His words refused to leave her head. She didn't want them to. She also needed him. But if she didn't take this deal, what then? Would she be any better off than when she'd had her every move monitored by her ex?

To the mediator Robin said, "May I please have a few moments of privacy to speak with my attorney?"

"Certainly. There's a conference area just through that door." She pointed to her right.

Marjorie rose, and Robin followed.

With the door closed behind them, Marjorie asked, "What are you doing? You've told me yourself that the Pierponts' ranch is enormous. You and Lark could spend a lifetime in their guesthouse and never even see them."

"But we would. All the time. What are my chances of winning this thing if I respectfully turn down Charlotte's offer?"

Her lawyer shrugged. "I would guess fairly good. But you never know in these kinds of cases. William's attorney did his best to paint you in an unflattering light and he pretty much succeeded. I'm not saying your falling for Laredo was wrong, but considering your background, it was way too fast."

"I know. I agree. But I'm fresh out of a marriage in which I spent every waking moment trying to please a man I abhorred. To now live under his parents' eagle eyes—I can't do it. Whether Laredo is in the equation or not, I can't do it. I won't."

"How do you feel about visitation?"

"I would never keep Charlotte—or even William from visiting Lark. All I want is to live my life without fear. Or judgment. But mostly, fear."

"I understand."

"Let's make Charlotte a counteroffer. One she hopefully won't refuse…"

"You owe me an explanation for that spectacle you made of both of us in court." Hours later, Robin stood in the open door of Laredo's motel room. From the looks of the open duffel bag on the bed, he was in the process of packing.

"Let it go. What's done is done, and I meant every word."

"Liar!" She slapped her palm hard enough against the open door to startle even herself. "What's wrong with you? Chuck's physical blows hurt less than the stunt you just pulled."

"You shouldn't be here." He wadded a T-shirt and pitched it into the gaping bag. "Where's Lark?"

"At the apartment with my grandparents. I told them I had to run out for diapers."

"So you won?"

"If you call having the man I thought I loved publicly dump and humiliate me a win, then yes."

"You've got your daughter. That's all that matters."

"Is it?"

He crammed his suit coat in the bag, followed by his dress shoes.

"Are you even listening to what I'm saying? I. Love. You." The hot afternoon sun felt as if it was burning a hole through her back. But there. She'd admitted the depth of her feelings for him. At least if he kept up this ridiculous story of never having felt anything for her, then she knew she'd done all she could to make things right between them. "I'm guessing your courthouse stunt was nothing more than a tool to force my decision, but that was something I never asked you to do."

He fished under the bed for his other dress shoe. "Glad it worked out for you."

"Could you at least do me the courtesy of looking at me?"

Standing upright, staring at the ceiling, he sighed. "I said everything I needed to in court."

"*Really?* That's really how you want to end this?"

"Yup." The stupid cowboy turned his back on her to head toward the bathroom, emerging with his toothbrush and toothpaste.

His phone chimed.

At the same time, a car pulled up outside his room.

"That's probably my Uber driver. To save time, I already turned in my rental car at a place around the corner."

Anger, frustration and inconceivable pain welled inside her. "This is about your night vision, isn't it? You think Lark and I could do better than hitching ourselves to a broken guy like you?"

After cramming the two halves of his bag together, he zipped it tight.

"You're not only an ass, but a coward. All you have to do for us to have a happy ending is admit that show back at the courthouse was for Charlotte's benefit, then open yourself up enough to let me in. I know you have feelings for me. I know what we shared wasn't all an act."

The driver honked the still-running car outside the room.

"Gotta go," he said.

Squeezing her hands into fists, swallowing the knot in her throat, she stepped aside to let him pass.

All of the beauty that had grown between them was now dead.

She wished she could say the same for her feelings.

At LAX, Laredo caught a flight to Denver, then a commuter flight back over the Rockies to land in Grand Junction. Once there, he called Jimmy for another huge favor in picking him up.

Twenty-eight hours later, he was home.

Robin must've called at least that many times. He'd let every call go to voice mail. Finally, the calls stopped.

His pain did not.

If he tried hard enough, he could pretend his whole adventure with Robin had never happened. Except for the fact that his bathroom smelled of her clean shampoo and floral lotion. Her bedroom still smelled of lemon oil and fresh linens and reminded him just how pleasant a tidy house could be.

Even worse was the goat pen.

Everywhere he looked he saw little Lark, giggling and laughing at the rowdy four-legged creatures. The concrete foundation had hardened. Lark's tiny handprint and perfectly penned name proved they'd existed. That for a brief few days, he'd been genuinely happy.

Now, he merely existed.

Felt numb.

Funny how this place used to be enough, trail rides with Chestnut used to make him feel whole, but now that he'd tasted the ambrosia of sharing his life with a woman who'd genuinely cared, he wanted more.

Putting on that show in front of the mediator and Robin's lawyer had damned near been the death of him.

Robin had known the score. He knew the moment Charlotte made her offer that the single mom would be forced to choose. In no way did he fault her decision.

Her daughter had to come first—always and forever.

The fact made him sad, but resolute in the rightness of his spur-of-the-moment act. His leaving had been noble. It had once again made him a hero—if only to himself.

Now, he sat on the porch swing nursing a beer, watching the sunset, readying himself to turn on every light in the house.

What he couldn't do was dwell on what might have been. He couldn't see Lark as a toddler, rescuing her from trouble as fast as she found it. He couldn't envision Robin standing at his stove, cooking them a delicious meal. He sure couldn't dream her into his bed, where the only thing she'd be wearing was the wedding ring he'd place on her finger.

"Hey, my little chicken. We're supposed to be getting the mail—not chasing butterflies."

Lark bucked in Robin's arms, pinching her chubby fingers in a valiant attempt to catch the graceful creature.

Robin tried helping by jogging her around the apartment complex's lush yard, but eventually the butterfly flew on his or her merry way.

"All gone," she said to her baby.

With the custody issue two months behind her, Robin should have been content. With Marjorie's help, she and Charlotte had worked out an open agreement, meaning she was welcome to visit Lark as often as she'd like. She loved taking her granddaughter on outings to the zoo and museums and lunch with her bridge club ladies. William had been slow to thaw but was gradually coming around. A big part of their improved relationship was the apology he'd made for looking the other way when he'd feared his son was following in his abusive footsteps yet had failed to get him help.

As part of her own healing, Robin was trying to forgive the father. All she'd ever feel was contempt for his son.

"Whew," she said to her chubby baby who was enjoying more and more solid foods. "We made it all the way to the mailbox." She slipped the key into her unit's box, then withdrew the day's delivery.

Electric bill.

Junk mail.

Junk mail.

Chinese delivery coupon.

Invitation? The black envelope sported Robin's name and an intricate silver calligraphy address on the front. On the back was an embossed silver return address. The name above it read: *Miss Sally DeHaven.*

Hands trembling, she rested Lark on her hip to open the surprise piece of mail. Inside was a Halloween-themed wedding invitation complete with candy-corn-shaped confetti. There was also a handwritten note.

*Hey girl!*
*Jimmy and I would love you even more if you'd drive over for the wedding. Sarah says she'll put you up in a complimentary room.*
*Let me know! xoxo*

Robin's mood turned melancholy.

Lark reached for the glittery invitation with its purple ghosts and jack-o'-lanterns.

"Pretty, huh?"

She let the baby have the thick card. Of course, Lark delivered it straight to her mouth.

Thinking about that brief turbulent time in her life produced a myriad of emotions. Robin still hadn't quite processed all of it, but she'd be forced to soon.

Some things were better said in person. Maybe going to the wedding would be the perfect time? She wasn't ready to face Laredo on his own. The fear his cruel words at that mediation session could have been the truth was all too real. Reinforced by his failure to answer any of her calls.

She'd thought she knew him so well.

Better than she'd known any man—especially, her ex-husband.

But what if she'd been wrong? What if her and Laredo's brief, happy time had all been an act on his part? What if his show of vulnerability had been an act?

He couldn't fake his night blindness.

*Ha!* Hadn't her time with Chuck proven anyone could fake anything?

She refused to believe Laredo could be anyone other than the hero she'd fallen for so hard and so fast. Regardless, he had his life and she had hers—twelve hours apart.

As soon as Lark entered preschool, Robin planned on returning to her work with special needs children. Maybe she'd even start on earning her teaching degree. Trudging up the stairs to her apartment, fighting a rush of nausea, she asked Lark, "Wanna take a nap with Mommy?"

The last place on earth Laredo wanted to be was at Jimmy and Sally's Halloween wedding, but since one of his groomsmen had come down with chicken pox, Laredo had been roped into standing in.

As a general rule, ever since his own marriage ended in disaster, he'd hated weddings. Having lost Robin, his hatred had grown tenfold.

But he'd made a promise and Jimmy was a good friend, so here he stood at the altar, witnessing vows between two people who would most likely be divorced in under five years.

*Knock it off,* his conscience scolded.

Once he got home he could be as gloomy as the cloudy day. Until then, he needed to suck it up and help the bride and groom enjoy their big event. Who knew? Maybe they'd buck the odds and be one of the lucky few who did live happily-ever-after.

While Jimmy stammered through his vows, and Sally and all of her bridesmaids cried through hers, he had to admit that they'd given the VFW hall one helluva spit-shine. The place had been decorated from top to bottom in black and orange balloons and streamers. Guests had been encouraged to come in costume. Jimmy campaigned hard for his groomsmen to dress as zombies, but Sally had shot down the idea on the grounds that she didn't want their future children to be too scared to look at their parents' wedding pictures.

Cue eye roll.

Good thing the VFW was within walking distance of The Lonely Cactus, so when he'd fulfilled his duties he could walk straight to bed—even if it was past dark.

The vows went on and on with singing and praying and more singing and then finally Pastor Paul—the same guy who'd reffed the chicken races Laredo watched with Robin—announced to the crowd, "It is a privilege to introduce our town's newest couple, Mr. and Mrs. Jimmy Schmidt."

The country band they'd hired for the afternoon and night broke into a twangy version of "Monster Mash."

When it came time for Laredo to join the procession, he took his assigned bridesmaid's arm, hooking it with his as instructed by the wedding planner.

The buxom brunette couldn't have been much over eighteen, but whispered, "I'm staying at the motel if you want to stop by later for beer. Room Fourteen."

"Thanks, but I'm busy."

"Your loss," she said at the end of the aisle.

He was forced to take group photos, rearrange chairs from wedding-mode rows to reception tables, then finally sidled up to the bar. The only good part of the brunette's offer had been the beer, but he'd rather put his latest on Jimmy's tab.

"Here you go," said the bartender—another of Jimmy's cousins.

"Thanks, man." Knowing it would be a long night, Laredo downed half the bottle in a few swigs.

A few too many Halloween songs later, he still stood at the bar when he caught a faint familiar floral scent.

"Where's your costume?" asked an instantly recognizable voice from behind him. *No way…*

He turned only to choke on his latest sip of beer.

Standing before him, wearing an adorable Little Bo Peep costume with Lark settled on her hip, dressed as a *sheep*, was Robin. She offered a shy smile. "Hey…"

"Hey, yourself. Why didn't you tell me you were coming?"

"Maybe I didn't know myself? Besides, it's not like you would have answered your phone."

Ouch. "How have you been?"

"Good. You?"

He shrugged before downing more brew. "I've been better. Been worse. Can't really complain. How are you liking life at the Pierponts'?"

"I'm not. Marjorie negotiated a better deal."

"Oh?" The news should have made him happy. Instead, it made him feel as if he'd given her up for nothing.

"I'm free to live my own life. My ex-in-laws are free to visit Lark as much as they like. I saw it as a win-win."

"Good. I'm glad you're happy."

She bowed her head. "I should be, right? Only...I'm not."

"Why?" His pulse raced and his breathing slowed, as he dared to hope the reason for her lackluster life involved missing him as much as he missed her.

Lark held out her arms to him, pinching her fingers.

"Hey, gorgeous." The baby gripped his pinkie finger. "You got so big."

"Looks like she remembers you."

"Mind if I hold her?"

"Not at all. But tell me one thing first."

"Shoot." He downed more beer.

"Those things you said at mediation. Did you mean them?"

"What do you think?"

Gaze shimmering, she shook her head.

"You'd be right. For my delivery style, I'm sorry. I never wanted to hurt you, but no way could I let you pass up that kind of opportunity."

"You mean living under my in-laws' thumbs?"

"I mean never worrying about a damned thing other than your child." He finished off his beer. Until this moment, he hadn't realized the full extent to which he'd missed her. Lark. He wanted to claim them both as his own. But clearly, she had no desire to be owned.

*Wonder if she'd want to be loved?*

As soon as the thought popped into his head, like a game of whack-a-mole he hammered it back down.

"What do you worry about, Laredo?"

"Lots of things." He signaled to the bartender for another beer, exchanging his empty for a full. "My goats and their kids being warm enough over the winter. My roof making it through the winter. My woodpile lasting through the—"

"Besides winter, what keeps you up at night?"

*You.*

*Missing you.*

*Wanting you.*

*Loving you.*

Lord help him, but he did love her. He didn't know how or why, but in some crazy twist of fate, they'd wound up together and he'd never wanted to let her go. Until he'd had to. And he'd been miserable every day since.

He blurted, "Ever think about me?"

"Honestly?" She grinned before shifting Lark to her other hip. "I try not to."

"Ouch. Way to bruise a guy's ego."

"You think about me?"

"Every. Single. Day."

His confession caused her big brown eyes to fill. "I have something to tell you." She was looking down again. "It's kind of big—well, not at the moment, but it will be. I don't want you to feel responsible, but you do need to know. That's why I'm here. To tell you my news."

His pounding heart threatened to implode.

Was she finally moving to Arkansas? Engaged? Moving to Arkansas with her new man? The guy with perfect day and night vision. The guy who didn't live on a ramshackle homestead out in the middle of nowhere but in a white house with a perfect picket fence.

Laredo *hated* that guy.

He envied that guy.

More than anything, he wanted to be that guy. Downing the rest of his beer, he said, "You and your new man have a great life. I really did enjoy our time together."

"What are you talking about? And just how many of those have you had?" She nodded toward his bottle.

"Lost count a while back."

"Well, you might want to sober up, cowboy."

"Why would I want to be sober when you're delivering shitty news?" He covered Lark's ears. "Sorry."

"Maybe I made the wrong decision in coming. I should have told you via snail mail."

"Told me what? Spit it out already."

"Not like this. I wanted, hoped—*prayed*—you'd be happy."

"Why would I be happy about you being with another guy?"

"Laredo—my news has nothing to do with another man. Unless I'm carrying your son. In which case, yes. There will soon be another very important guy in my life. Until then, you're going to have to do."

"Hold up..." He used his bottle to tip back his cowboy hat, then press the cold, sweating side to his suddenly too-hot forehead. "Did you just say what I think you did?"

Silent tears falling, she nodded. "I'm pregnant. And as much as I don't want to, I miss you. I miss laughing with you and fighting with you and...kissing you."

He set his bottle down on the bar to draw her and Lark into a hug. *"I love you,"* he said, pressing a kiss to her forehead. *"I love you,"* he said after kissing the tip of her nose. *"I love you,"* he said to each of her cheeks. He kissed Robin's lips before telling Lark how much he loved her, too. "I'm so sorry for my courtroom stunt and for just now thinking you'd run off with another guy. It's just that... I love you."

"You may have mentioned that." Her grin lifted him higher than a dozen more beers.

All around them the reception grew rowdy.

The band blared honky-tonk and most every cowboy, ghost and fairy in the hall was already well beyond the legal limit. But for Laredo, suddenly the only two people in the room—in his world—were Robin and Lark.

And his baby. *His baby!*

He dropped to his knees, kissing Robin's still-flat belly. "I love you, too."

*"Laredo..."*

"That's me..." Still drunk on beer and life and his two girls, he grinned before standing, slipping his arms around her waist, drawing her close. "I know we barely know each other, and given our past crap luck in love, this is probably a lousy idea, but would you do me the honor of becoming my wife?"

Laughing, crying, she said, "This is probably a really bad idea, but *yes*!"

# Epilogue

Robin drew back the kitchen curtain and shook her head.

She was thrilled to have such a large turnout for her first Fourth of July celebration on the homestead, but if William and her grandfather didn't stop trying to one-up each other, one or both would wind up hurt.

Her grandparents' wedding gift had been to renovate the shed into a darling guesthouse that they used every couple of months when they visited.

Not to be outdone, the Pierponts had gifted a swimming pool complete with a diving board and slide. Both family patriarchs now stood alongside the diving board, goading each other to do more outrageous dives.

Luckily, Charlotte and her grandmother stepped in, pulling them to opposite sides of the pool.

"When do we get the house to ourselves again?" Laredo stepped up from behind her, holding sleeping two-month-old Clint in his arms. They'd named him after her deceased father.

"I'm afraid it's going to be a while and I need to study." In between caring for the kids and garden and lovingly restoring the historic home, Robin was taking online classes to earn her teaching degree. "Now that your parents bought the RV, I'm afraid they'll be parked here indefinitely."

He groaned.

Also in attendance were his two big brothers and their families. Augusta and Ned, Jimmy and Sally, even Lulu and Sarah, who were flirting with every eligible bachelor—mostly Jimmy's cousins.

After nuzzling her neck, her husband asked, "Do you ever think about how far we've come in such a short time and feel blessed?"

"Every minute of every day—until Charlotte and Grandma take cues from their one-upping husbands and spoil Lark. What is Grandma giving her now?" They'd moved to the pool's fence to greet a man leading a pony.

"Is that Kyle?" Laredo asked.

"He didn't… He wouldn't…"

"I'm afraid he did bring our toddler a pony. Now the only question is which of the grandmothers in her life put him up to it?"

Now, Robin groaned. "Do we have to go back out there? Looks like everything's kind of under control. I just want a nap."

"Mind if I join you?"

She grinned. "You know if you're with me, the last thing we'll be doing is napping?"

"Yep. Why else did you think I asked?" He winked.

"Let me slip this guy into his crib, then meet me between the sheets. Or on top—I'm not choosy."

As usual when her husband propositioned her, she swooned. And then waited for him to join her in their bedroom…

* * * * *

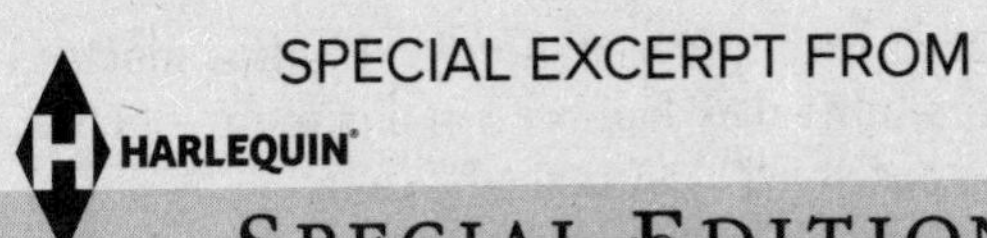


*To give the orphaned triplets they're guardians of the stability they need, Lulu McCabe and Sam Kirkland decide to jointly adopt them. But when it's discovered their marriage wasn't actually annulled, they have to prove to the courts they're responsible—by renewing their vows!*

*Read on for a sneak preview of Cathy Gillen Thacker's* Their Inherited Triplets, *the next book in the Texas Legends: The McCabes miniseries.*

"The two of you are still married," Liz said.

"Still?" Lulu croaked.

Sam asked, "What are you talking about?"

"More to the point, how do you know this?" Lulu demanded, the news continuing to hit her like a gut punch.

Travis looked down at the papers in front of him. "Official state records show you eloped in the Double Knot Wedding Chapel in Memphis, Tennessee, on Monday, March 14, nearly ten years ago. Alongside another couple, Peter and Theresa Thompson, in a double wedding ceremony."

Lulu gulped. "But our union was never legal," she pointed out, trying to stay calm, while Sam sat beside her in stoic silence.

Liz countered, "Ah, actually, it is legal. In fact, it's still valid to this day."

Sam reached over and took her hand in his, much as he had the first time they had been in this room together. "How is that possible?" Lulu asked weakly.

"We never mailed in the certificate of marriage, along with the license, to the state of Tennessee," Sam said.

"And for our union to be recorded and therefore legal, we had to have done that," Lulu reiterated.

"Well, apparently, the owners of the Double Knot Wedding Chapel did, and your marriage was recorded. And is still valid to this day, near as we can tell. Unless you two got a divorce or an annulment somewhere else? Say another country?" Travis prodded.

"Why would we do that? We didn't know we were married," Sam returned.

*Don't miss*
Their Inherited Triplets *by Cathy Gillen Thacker,*
*available August 2019 wherever*
*Harlequin® Special Edition books and ebooks are sold.*

www.Harlequin.com



HSEEXP0719